GIRL ON THE FLY

Also by Nansubuga Nagadya Isdahl

Beyoncé (First Names)
Nelson (First Names)

GIRL ON THE FLY

Nansubuga
Nagadya Isdahl

David Fickling Books

Girl on the Fly
is a
DAVID FICKLING BOOK

First published in Great Britain in 2024 by
David Fickling Books,
31 Beaumont Street,
Oxford, OX1 2NP

Text © Nansubuga Nagadya Isdahl, 2024

978-1-788451-84-0

1 3 5 7 9 10 8 6 4 2

Papers used by David Fickling Books are from well-
managed forests and other responsible sources.

DAVID FICKLING BOOKS Reg. No. 8340307

A CIP catalogue record for this book is available from the British Library.

Typeset in Sabon LT Pro by Falcon Oast Graphic Art Ltd.
Printed and bound in Great Britain by Clays Ltd, Elcograf S.p.A.

For Joy, Nsaba, Esperanza and Imani,
our girls poised to soar!

HEARTBEATS

Baba says when I was small, I was always on the hunt for heartbeats. I'd snuggle in his arms, clamouring to hear the steady *boom*, *boom*, *boom* beating from somewhere deep in his chest. The story goes I would try to find the sound of a heartbeat just about everywhere. Anywhere. Baba also likes to say that if I'd been born in Tanzania, like him, he would have taken me to the family farm with its millions of goats and chickens and cows, and I would have found way more heartbeats than I knew what to do with.

But that's just Baba being Baba!

Instead of chasing farm animals, I used to cup my hand behind my ear and press it against tree trunks. Flower petals. My dolls and my trucks. Even the dirt-caked soles of Odie's feet. That was before we grew up and grew out of that kind of stuff. And obviously before I truly understood what a heart was. Or where to find one.

Truth be told, I don't actually remember hunting for heartbeats.

My memories don't reach that far back.

What I *do* remember is what happened when I started running. That's when I became a hurricane of arms and feet and one gigantic heartbeat.

BOOM! BOOM! BOOM!

It's also when Alexis, Neeka, Luce and I started flying around the track, *smack*, *smack*, *smack*, smacking a baton into the palms of each other's hands.

When we forgot everything, except our rhythm and flow.

When we found freedom . . . and the thrill of soaring across the finish line.

Thinking back on it now, though, I wonder. When I was small and searching everywhere and anywhere, in every little thing, for that steady *boom*, *boom*, *boom*, what exactly did I think I was looking for?

PART ONE:

ON YOUR MARKS

Philadelphia 1992

1.
SOMETHING EXTRA

'We don't need something extra,' Neeka said with her chest puffed up. 'We're fast . . . *remember*? Plus, we're thirteen.' She tilted her head towards the sun, which was just starting to slant down low. Bronze shadows cut lines across the red-brick wall behind her.

It was a Friday afternoon in April, and we were the last girls on the track. Since practice was done for the day, I thought Neeka would be easier to convince. But her hands stayed glued to her hips. Her face wouldn't give either.

Level ten hard-headedness.

'Trust me,' I said, squaring my shoulders. 'We do.'

Being fast wasn't enough.

And even though we'd been counting down the days until Luce finally turned thirteen – she was the last one in the group – that wouldn't cut it either.

If we wanted to win our relay race at the two biggest track meets of the season – *our last two races together* – something extra was a must.

'What about our race day nicknames?' Luce asked, smacking her lips like her bubble gum was lunch. 'Those *gotta* count?' She was sitting down in front of us on the thick white line that split lanes four and five. Her tube socks, hiked up all the way to her kneecaps, made her look even tinier than she already was.

'Nope. Don't count,' I said. 'First, we've had those nicknames since fifth grade. If they held any drop of extra luck, we'd be state champions by now. Second, we need something with more flair. Something with rhythm and a beat to it. Something supersonic!'

Luce looked at me. Her right eyebrow rose.

She shimmied her pint-sized shoulders, I slid my steps and we shouted out in unison just like the J.J. Fad song.

Luce loved that old song even more than I did.

We could dance all day every day to it.

One Saturday last year we *did* dance all day to it.

I could hardly bear to think about Luce moving away at the end of summer.

Who else had clown antics to keep me in stitches?

No one.

Alexis was too Alexis.

And Neeka? She was only silly when the Holy Spirit moved her.

Which was never.

Luckily, when we ran the 4 x 100 relay, none of that mattered.

On the track, we moved like rhythm and beat rolled into one.

And with Luce leaving, this championship season would be our last time to flow together.

So, losing wasn't an option. We had to win.

And we had to win BIG.

That's why we *really* needed something special!

While Luce cracked a million more Bazooka bubbles, Alexis jogged over, cool as a breeze. She was the last of us to finish. But she must've caught snatches of our conversation on her last loop because here she was, slipping in her two cents.

'What we *need*,' Alexis said, the words gliding right out of her mouth, 'is some majestic flyness.' She reached her hand up and pushed a bobby pin deeper into the bun coiled tightly on top of her head. Then she licked her fingers and smoothed down her baby hairs. 'That's how we win the 4 x 100 relay this year.'

And winning was everything!

2.
MAJESTIC FLYNESS

Technically, the four of us – me, Neeka, Alexis and Luce – had placed before.

Lots of *second* places.

I thought about the picture of Flo-Jo I had tacked up on my bedroom wall.

The fastest woman on earth.

Her 4 x 100 relay team *had* won first place. And not just *any* first place.

They'd struck gold four years ago at the 1988 Olympics, half-way across the world in Seoul. Flo-Jo had her 'something extra' in spades.

Six-inch gold nails that turned into mini-magic wands.

They helped her cut through the wind.

And her one-legged track suits sent her flying like a blazing comet.

She was majestic flyness in motion. She had to be.

Because nobody remembered who came in second.

And I wanted the four of us to remember each other forever.

'Majestic flyness,' Neeka said, repeating Alexis but staring straight at me. She finally dropped her hands from her hips and nodded her head. 'Now that's what I'm talking about.' The gold specks in her green eyes jumped around like fireflies, which meant she'd finally turned the corner from hard-headed.

I frowned. 'Isn't that what I said?'

'No,' Neeka answered back. 'You said something extra, which is like a soggy side of fries.' Luce stifled a laugh.

I shook my head. 'No, it's—'

'Can you two stop and let me finish?' Alexis said, speaking over me. Her eyes brightened. 'Here's my idea. We need a song.' Then she leaned back and spread her hands wide, like her grand idea had been written in the sky.

'A rap?' Luce asked, from down below. All three of us put our hands on our hips and made the same exact slow roll in her direction.

'A song, not a rap, Luce,' Alexis corrected in her teacher's voice.

'Maybe a chant,' I said, slowly nodding my head.

We grabbed our gear and started walking towards the school.

'That's it,' Alexis said to me, shoving my shoulder. 'A chant. You could write it, too. The way you map everything out . . . and go on and on ad nauseam about rhythm.'

'Ad *who*?' Luce asked, her eyes ballooning.

9

Alexis smirked, at me or Luce I didn't know, but I knew she was right. I had blueprints in my mind for a world of things. I guess because I liked knowing exactly how things were going to begin and how they were going to end.

I loved things that flowed, too.

Songs flowed. But chants?

They had a special kind of rhythm all their own.

Momma spoke chants sometimes with her women's circle.

But those weren't the right kind.

My mind flashed to the only other time I'd heard one live.

It happened when Baba took me to a high school basketball game.

I was sitting on the edge of the bleachers with my head buried in my knees. My fingers were reaching for the laces of my high-tops, making a special loop so they stayed tied tight. Out of the corner of my eye, I saw the away team march in. Only thing is, they started spelling out their team's name in unison, eyes straight ahead, clapping and stomping to their own beat as they made their way to the bench.

H – *clap, clap, stomp, clap*

A – *clap, clap, stomp, clap*

W – *clap, clap, stomp, clap*

K – *clap, clap, stomp, clap*

H – clap, clap, stomp, clap

O – clap, clap, stomp, clap

U – clap, clap, stomp, clap

S – clap, clap, stomp, clap

E – clap, clap, stomp, clap

They filled the whole gym with their sound.

It floated high above the hardwood floors all the way to the rafters.

This wasn't some ordinary cheer. It was like their very own battle cry.

They'd put a stamp on it.

I swear even the fluorescent lights shone brighter. I'm pretty sure the home team got the message too. Because they quit passing balls back and forth and stood awestruck.

Hawk House had conjured up something really special.

And when they won, you think anyone was surprised?

Of course not.

The chant was that extra magic touch that pulled their team together and kept them focused. It was so powerful I still remembered it vibrating through my entire body. It was maybe even so powerful it would keep Hawk House bonded for life. I snaked my arm around Luce's neck as we reached the double doors. A cool blast of air hit my face as I walked in and tried to keep the wheels in my head from spinning too fast. By the time I hefted my backpack over my shoulder and we walked out of the locker room, I was sure.

I'd write something like that for us.

Something that would help us steady our steps and stay in sync.

Something that would guarantee our greatness and send us straight across the state championship finish line in first place . . .

Something none of us would ever forget!

3.
T MINUS
TWO WEEKS

After practice, I made a mad dash home. The regional championship meet was only two weeks away. The big state meet would follow soon after. I didn't have a whole lot of time to conjure up something solid gold. Especially from scratch.

The plan was simple.

When I got home, I'd dodge Momma, tear up the stairs to my desk, and wait for the magic to pour from my mind like a fountain of wisdom.

We'd be ready for the championship meets in no time.

That *was* the plan.

But as soon as I thundered through the front door and started to unlace my sneakers, I saw problem number one: Momma wasn't there to dodge. She should've been standing in the front hall, tap-tap-tappity-tapping her foot and snapping at me for the mess I was just about to make.

I walked to the kitchen door and poked my head around. That's when I saw problem number two: no snack waiting for me on the table. No kettle on the stove. In this house, there was *always* a kettle screaming at five p.m. Five-thirty at the latest on the days Momma had a straggling client.

Today, though?

Nothing.

I followed the sound of hushed voices to Baba's study.

That's when I saw problem number three. The *real* problem: three adults talking super sly.

'I'm sorry to hear that,' Aunt Darien said.

Aunt Darien and Momma had been best friends since forever. Long before I was born. Aunt Darien's son, Odie, was my best friend, too. Or at least he was until our friendship suddenly screeched to a halt earlier this year. I still hadn't figured out exactly how to fix it.

'Us, too,' Momma said in a serious voice. 'It's very sad. And she's such a lovely girl. Well, she's a woman now, really, with her own kids.' Her shoulders rose and fell in a sigh. 'This must be so hard on the kids.'

'I'm sure it is,' Aunt Darien said. 'How many does she have?'

'Three,' Momma answered back.

'But the kids are in boarding school so they will stay in Tanzania. Only Rose is coming.' That was Baba piping in. He leaned over from his desk, where he was sitting, and clasped his hands just as I slunk in.

'Coming?' I asked, extra quiet.

Three heads turned towards me.

Momma glanced down at her watch and then looked back at me like I'd beamed down straight from Mars.

A thick silence hung in the air while everyone stayed still.

It was the kind of stillness that shook and the kind of silence that screamed.

Aunt Darien spoke first. 'Such a lovely surprise to see you, Kam.' She looked from Momma to Baba, pressed her hands into her knees, and stood up from the couch. She walked over and planted a kiss on my cheek. 'You need to come over more. I haven't heard you and Odie and your ear-splitting music in a while.'

I guess she didn't know how much things had changed.

How out of step Odie and I were now.

I looked down at my feet. 'Yeah . . . I guess we aren't hanging out as much.'

Aunt Darien slung her purse around her shoulder and smiled. 'I never thought I'd say this but . . . I'd love more of your loudness. I know you're busy, but make sure I see you . . . or at least hear you soon.' She turned to Baba and Momma. 'And if you guys need any help with your visitor, just shout. You know where to find me. Hopefully her visit will be the end of the family trouble.' She gave me a tight squeeze before she walked out, while I chewed my lip.

Trouble?

4.
CLASSIC

I just knew it. That stillness *had* screamed. As soon as I heard the heavy thud of the front door shutting, I turned to Momma and Baba and cut to the chase. 'What trouble?'

Baba loosened the knot in his tie.

He rolled his leather chair away from his desk and stood to face me.

It was almost like looking in the mirror.

Same long face. Same almond eyes. Same long fingers.

Only difference was Baba's brown ran deeper.

And he was a tall I wished never to be.

'Lucky you,' Momma had whispered in my ear once. We were taking a long Sunday walk along the river. It was dark, and the path in front of us twinkled from the lights that lined Boathouse Row. I remember the crunching of our steps moving over a bed of dead leaves. When I asked Momma why I was so lucky, she pointed at Baba, who was footsteps ahead, and said, 'Because you look like

16

your Baba.' Through the eyes of Momma's thick love, no one was more handsome than Baba.

And it was true. People often looked twice when he passed by. I didn't feel so lucky, though. The only thing I saw when I looked in the mirror was a stick.

'Well,' Momma said now, pulling me down onto the sofa. 'Maybe Baba should start.' Baba came over from his desk and sat down on my other side. He leaned forward with his elbows on his knees, his hands clasped together tight.

He took one of my hands into his. Momma took my other hand and squeezed it. I glanced down at Baba's smooth, dark hand and Momma's milky white, blue-veined one.

Outside of meals, the three of us hadn't sat together like this in a while. Mostly because Baba's head was buried in a big case. He barely had time to talk these days. I guess today was an exception.

Baba started. 'Your Aunt Rose is going through a hard time right now and she needs a break. We've invited her to come stay with us for a while.'

'Oh,' I squeaked out, sinking back further into the couch. I started to hunt through my mind, searching for the few files I had on Baba's family back in Tanzania.

Aunt Rose.

I knew she was Baba's younger sister.

I had a hard time conjuring up her image, though.

I'm sure I'd seen her picture in the family album, but we'd never met before.

17

I'd spoken to her exactly one time on the phone. That was a few years ago. The line kept cutting out and her accent was as thick as the *ugali* Baba always tried (and failed) to get me to eat.

I knew she had three kids. One girl and twin boys.

And, apparently, she was in some kind of trouble.

I sighed, the chant niggling at the back of my mind like an itch I couldn't scratch.

My leg started to bounce, bounce, bounce up and down. Faster and faster.

Momma patted my thigh. 'I know. It's terrible.'

I nodded, feeling a little uneasy. I'd been thinking about myself and not Aunt Rose.

'But don't worry,' Momma said way too chipper. 'She'll be fine.' She smiled. 'As for you, we know you don't like change. I still remember when you were at Bright Star Montessori and I had to—'

'*Yeah, yeah*, I know.' I shook my head. 'I wouldn't let you leave on the first day of school or the days after that, and Ms Delinah was nice enough to let you do your paperwork from her office for two whole months until I got "acclimated".'

'And then you adjusted beautifully. You always do.'

Not really, I thought. I was still the girl who liked things that were familiar and who needed a minute to adjust to sudden change.

OK. Maybe more than a minute.

Way more.

'So . . .' I started. 'What kind of trouble is she in?'

Baba closed his eyes and pinched the bridge of his nose. He inhaled so deep I was afraid he was going to suck up all the oxygen in the room. 'It's a very delicate situation.'

Momma and Baba went on to explain that Aunt Rose had called them up and told them her husband had left her a month ago. Momma said he'd been causing her all kinds of trouble.

Bad-to-the-bone kind of trouble. He'd gone to work one morning and never came back.

Vanished like a ghost, leaving her with three kids. She needed some time to figure out her next steps. Baba, forever the lawyer, called it an open-and-shut case. She was family. Of course, they'd help her out.

I shifted nervously in my seat. 'That sounds bad. Really bad.' I paused for a second. Drummed my fingers on my thighs. 'So how long is she staying with us?'

I couldn't help but ask. A lot was riding on the last few weeks of school.

The girls and I *had* to win the state track championship. And I had to write a winning chant to make sure it happened.

Fixing things with Odie nagged at me, too.

It felt like a huge weight, bringing me down.

My thoughts started to swarm.

How would I be able to focus on winning the biggest races of the season – our last shot before Luce moved away – with a new person in the house suddenly changing my rhythm?

I couldn't let anything stand in the way of our winning. Not when it mattered this much.

After a long while, Baba finally spoke. 'You don't ask guests how long they are staying, Kamaria. Especially family. And most especially family in need.'

I drew in a deep breath, thinking about what I really needed to know, and then spit it out. 'Can you at least tell me where she's going to sleep?'

Baba scratched the crook of his elbow and looked at me like I'd temporarily lost my mind. 'We've just told you that your aunt's family has fallen apart and you're worried about sharing a room?'

Yeah . . . well, technically, I didn't know her. So . . . I thought it was a fair question.

'Not exactly,' I said, finding a crumb of sense before the thoughts in my head tumbled out. 'I just wanted to know what to expect. You know, the implications.'

Baba's word of the year.

Consider the implications of not telling the whole story, Kamaria.

Kamaria, there are implications for others when you don't show up on time.

Well, I wanted to know what the implications of Aunt Rose's visit were. Baba, the lawyer, master of logic, should have been able to connect all the dots, like I was doing right now.

Wasn't it obvious?

If Aunt Rose moved into my room, she could ruin my focus.

She could be loud and bossy or messy and fussy.

Wait . . . She could hijack everything.

The chant. Our winning. That moment we would never forget.

Aunt Rose was DEFINITELY going to turn my whole world upside down.

I sighed deeply.

Instead of working out the math like I did, Baba said, 'The implications are far greater for her than they are for you.'

Classic Baba vagueness.

'Flexibility, Kam. Think flexible,' Momma chimed, giving my hand another hard squeeze.

Classic Momma smoothness.

I nodded and kept my mouth shut. I knew what flexible meant.

It was code for get ready to share a room.

And there was more.

The trouble just kept stacking up.

She was coming on Sunday.

In two days!

5.
THINGS THAT GO BOOM

A few hours later I was freshly showered and my thoughts were still swarming. I sank deeper into my bed and stared at the five Olympic rings on my bedroom ceiling. When I first started running, Momma stencilled them and Odie helped me paint them in hot pink and baby blue.

Looking at them usually got me jazzed . . . or kept me focused.

Not tonight.

All I could see was Aunt Rose on a plane to Philly, her flight path headed straight for my life. I got a knot in the pit of my stomach, hoping she wouldn't crash land into me . . . or my big plans.

My mind leaped to Odie and the way things were before we fell out of step.

Friday night marathon phone calls.

Saturday night TV shows, our limbs splayed out on my living room floor.

Sunday afternoon pit stops at our favorite ice cream parlour, Carmichael's Creamery.

Monday morning school pick-ups, when he would tap on the stained-glass part of the front door three times at 7:15 a.m. on the dot, then wait for me on the stoop. Five minutes later, he'd still be waiting and would shout, 'Come on, slow poke. I can hear you. Hurry up!' I'd smile from the other side of the door and shout back, 'Coming!' and when I slid out, he'd be pacing. Sometimes I took so long we'd have to book it to school, our backpacks whacking hard against our backs.

Talking and laughing and cone crunching.

Tapping and shouting and dashing and whacking.

The sound of us . . . until things went *boom*.

The more I waded into the memories, the more I realized it wasn't helping.

Thinking about the good only reminded me of the bad.

Things were so bad now that when I saw Odie in the hallways at school, he usually turned around and started scrambling in the other direction. Any chance I had to talk to him about how to handle the Aunt Rose situation *before* she landed on our doorstep was out of the question, too.

My leg started twitching under the bedsheet.

Turns out wishing I could talk to Odie was even worse than thinking about Aunt Rose's visit.

I changed gear completely and tried looking at what my eyes could actually see.

My bookshelf carefully lined with track ribbons and school awards.

Momma's old globe sitting on my desk, tilted like the actual earth. It was even raised a little higher where the mountains were so you could trace the ridges with your fingers. My eyes passed over my CDs, neatly stacked, before eventually landing above my desk, on the framed magazine cover with Flo-Jo and Jackie Joyner-Kersee.

Six Olympic medals between them.

Flo-Jo wasn't running in this year's games, but it didn't matter.

She was already a first-rate champion.

A legend.

A magic-maker.

I tried picturing myself standing right beside her, holding up a gold medal of my own. But the image fizzled away too soon.

Time was creeping by and sleep still wasn't coming easy so I hiked the covers up high over my head like I'd done a million times before and tried listening for the one thing that might actually make me feel better.

The one thing I could hear crystal clear.

The one thing that always sounded right.

The sound of the four of us winning!

It helped that I'd been repeating the words in my mind for a whole year:

Alexis Evans shoots out of the block in the lead. There is nothing to stand in her way. A perfect pass to Kamaria Kessy who doesn't give an inch and widens the gap. Luce

Vidal kicks up dust as she takes the curve. And Daneeka Davenport brings it all the way home! She raises her arms as she crosses the finish line. The River Park Middle School girls' 4 x 100 relay team wins first place. And it only gets better.

They broke their own record.
And the state record!
The girls fall to the ground.
The crowd stomps their feet!
The metal bleachers go BOOM, BOOM, BOOM.

6.
PLAN A

I woke up on Saturday morning with a fresh bout of dread.

'Momma?' I shouted out, dragging myself downstairs.

Nothing.

I called for her again as I walked through the hallway into the living room.

She wasn't there, but the house was spotless.

I looked around at the crisp set of tracks in the carpet. A sign Momma had vacuumed it to death. Bright yellow tulips nodded happily in their vases. I walked back to Momma's office and almost bowled her over on the way.

She'd been walking with her head down, muttering to herself and not paying any attention whatsoever. She was wearing her signature cleaning get-up: highwater jeans, a white V-neck T-shirt, pink flip-flops, and floppy yellow rubber gloves that hit her elbows. A black bandana held her bouncy hair back.

When she finally looked up, the gaze in her eyes was intense.

'What were you doing?' I asked, crossing my arms over my chest.

'Finishing touches,' she said.

'For what?' I asked, half-jokingly.

She looked at me with exasperation. 'Aunt Rose is coming tomorrow night!'

How could I forget?

I was the one who was going to be sleeping next to her.

A relative I'd never met.

A relative whose strange habits or moods could distract me from getting in the zone and cranking out a champion-level chant.

And this time I didn't have jokey Odie to lighten things up and help me focus.

He usually helped me see past whatever my problem was so I could find a fix.

At least I'd made another plan.

A plan B.

Or, really, a plan A . . .

A for Alexis.

I sighed and gave Momma a weak smile. 'But Alexis can still spend the night tonight and help me get my room ready right?'

My head, too.

'Of course,' she said putting her rubber-gloved hands on my shoulders and marching me into the kitchen. 'But first, I need your help with a little something.' Momma had a smooth way of enrolling you in things you never had any mind to do and before you knew it, the sun was sliding from the sky and your own plans were in the toilet. Even worse, I was right about Aunt Rose. She wasn't even here yet and she was already side-tracking things and slowing me down.

7.
NO PRIVACY
NO PEACE

'Look at what I found!' Baba said as he waltzed through the kitchen door a few hours later. His eyes were gleaming, even though he was coming in from a long day of work. He dropped a huge, spiky green blob on the table.

'Oh, yum!' Alexis said excitedly. 'Jackfruit.'

Alexis and I were sitting at the kitchen table watching Momma at the stove and hoping she wouldn't burn the plantain. Or set the house on fire.

'I knew you'd appreciate my surprise,' Baba said to Alexis, with a satisfied look. Anytime Alexis spent the night, he always tried to bring home something 'African'. Her family was from Barbados and ate a lot of the same foods we did. 'We'll eat some and save a bit for Rose.'

He took off his blue blazer and carefully draped it on a chair. Then he walked over to the fridge and poured a glass of water.

I sank down low into my seat.

Plan A hadn't quite worked out yet. It was already dinner time and Alexis and I had done exactly zero work on my room. I still hadn't gotten used to the idea of an Aunt Rose, either. We had watched about eight hours of music videos non-stop, though.

Alexis had tried to wave away my worries while we clicked back and forth between VH1 and MTV. 'Aunt Rose is gonna be dope, not distracting,' she said, her cheeks bulging with chips.

I tilted my head suspiciously at her. 'And you know this how?'

But the 'My Lovin'' video from En Vogue whipped across the screen and she was too busy moving in her seat and licking salt from her fingers to answer.

Odie would have come back with something silly.

The perfect thing to distract me from myself.

He was always there when I needed him.

At least, that's how it used to be.

I didn't have a big family like Alexis or Luce or Neeka with siblings and legions of cousins. It had always just been the three of us: Me, Momma and Baba.

Plus Odie.

He was a big part of us too.

Baba took Odie and me skiing in Vermont every winter and camping in the Poconos every summer. For sleepovers, I had my own lumpy pillow at his house. He had his own set of chores at mine.

I guess it wasn't just the thought of having no privacy

and no peace to write the chant that worried me. I was also nervous about having someone else around the house all the time. Of course, I always made an exception for my friends.

Like Alexis tonight.

Normally, though, the fourth seat at the kitchen table was for Odie. So was the spare bed and every other extra thing in the house.

How would Aunt Rose fit into this picture?

My gut tightened.

I looked up from the table and asked, 'Do you think jackfruit from Tanzania and jackfruit from Barbados taste the same?' I'd never tasted it before and from the look of it, I wasn't sure I was ready to try.

'I don't know if the varieties from Tanzania and Barbados are the same,' Baba answered. 'But I found this one at the Haitian store, so I guess we're going to find out how it tastes there.'

Momma, looking worn out, swiped a lock of hair out of her face. Then she reached over the kitchen island and handed Baba the plate of fried plantain. They were resting on top of a grease-soaked paper towel. They were burnt.

Momma couldn't cook to save her life. When Odie and I were little, we used to call her hard-boiled eggs 'char-boiled' eggs. Then we'd wait for Baba to serve us something safe to eat. He'd still be the one cooking our meals now if it wasn't for his big case. Momma only started stepping up to the plate this year. I just hoped our brownstone didn't burn down in the meantime.

Baba carried the plate of scorched plantain to the table and placed it next to the rest of the sketchy-looking food. He took his seat and pulled Momma's away from the table. 'Let's dive in,' he said, smiling.

Momma thumped down in her seat. 'Yes, let's,' she mumbled.

I gave her a thumbs up and braced myself.

Baba handed Alexis a plate and went to town, lecturing us on how food is culture.

'Thank you, Mr Kessy,' Alexis said, looking Baba straight in the eye and nodding respectfully at his every word. I knew Alexis would eat all her food no matter how singed it was because she was a fanatic about having good manners. And good manners were first on the long list of things about Tanzania that Baba was always hollering about. It was always a big show.

Tonight, it was even worse.

It went something like this . . .

Back home in Tanzania, we raise our kids to be well-mannered.

Back home in Tanzania, we eat real food, not from packets.

Back home in Tanzania, students wear school uniforms, not sweat suits.

Back home in Tanzania, there's no such thing as a 'nerd' – doing well makes you popular!

Normally, I'd just tune Baba out when he was on a roll.

But listening to the deep in his voice tonight, I could

hear something different. It was like he was even more proud. Probably because Aunt Rose was coming.

Wait?

Was this what I had to look forward to?

Two adults tag-teaming lectures . . .

And talking in parables . . .

And giving life lessons . . .

And spreading the *Back home in Tanzania* gospel . . .

Baba was still rambling, and I tried to tune back in, but when I swallowed, I nearly choked on a clump of charred rice. I put my hand to my throat and looked around to see if anyone was checking for me.

They weren't.

Not even Alexis, who was still shovelling food into her mouth.

I hoped Aunt Rose wasn't planning to slip into a spot at this table all easy breezy.

Even if she was family.

As far as I was concerned, every seat was already taken.

8.
FORMERLY
KNOWN AS . . .

'Do you think I should move my bed the long way?' I asked Alexis. 'That way we won't be side to side.' We had just narrowly escaped another boring Baba story in the kitchen and were upstairs in my bedroom, plotting.

I sat on my bed with my legs crossed.

Alexis sat on the bed across from me.

Aunt Rose's bed now.

'If you move the bed that way . . .' Alexis got up and walked around the room, measuring the space with her arm span. 'Then you won't have any space in the middle.'

I sighed.

'Just move that *overrrrr*,' she sang, mimicking the Sybil song. She jerked her thumb in the direction of my bookshelf.

I started to pick at a loose thread on my comforter. 'Since when do you sing?'

'Since you're gonna need some help with our chant.'

'And why do you think that?'

'Because your "Aunt Rose this and Aunt Rose that" is already taking up all your headspace and she hasn't even landed.' She started grinning slyly. 'But you'll tell me the minute you have something written down right? I can't wait to jam. And I definitely can't wait for us to finally snatch that first-place win.' She came over to me with her hand raised high and waited for me to smack it back.

'Well,' I said, wiggling around and ignoring her question and her high five because I had absolutely nothing good to show. 'If you did your job and distracted me, I'd be able to forget about Aunt Rose and focus on writing something perfect.'

She shooed me away like I was a fly. Then she walked over to the bookshelf and picked up a framed picture of me and Odie in kindergarten. She turned back around towards me. 'I'm here to help you not distract you. Who do you think I am? Your best friend, Odie?' She smiled, holding the picture to her heart.

The thread I was picking at unravelled even further. I flopped over on my back and folded my arms behind my head, feeling a prick of heat spread all over my body. 'I think you mean Odie, formerly known as my best friend. You know we're still not talking.'

'Yeah, I know,' she said, looking at me cockeyed. 'But it still doesn't make sense. You two have been friends since the *Mayflower* set sail.' She brandished the frame like it was somehow proof of us as Pilgrim Fathers, then returned it to the bookshelf and flounced back down on the other bed. The mattress bounced a little. She propped her elbows on her knees and her fists under her chin. Her face got all soft. 'Come on, Kam, what *really* happened?'

9.
CHAOS TO
MY COSMOS

I cradled my head in my hands, squeezed my eyes shut, and blew out a sigh. A few seconds later, when my eyes popped open, Alexis was still sitting on the bed patiently waiting for my answer.

'Honestly, I don't know what happened,' I said. 'We stopped eating lunch together, I guess.'

'So, for real? That was it? You two clowns stopped being friends because of lunch?' Alexis picked up a stuffed animal from the bed and squeezed the life out of it. 'Makes no sense.'

It still didn't make sense to me either.

'I guess he just got mad at me and that was that.'

Alexis flipped her hair over her head and grabbed it into the scrunchie that was wrapped around her wrist. Then, she shifted herself a bit to get more comfortable.

Her huge bamboo earrings glinted under the lights.

I eyed them with envy.

'But why don't you ask him again? Like, "Odie, it's been a while. What's up?" Then you can end this mystery episode once and for all.' Alexis had started calling my rift with Odie the Great Mystery Episode because she said it was even more ridiculous than an episode of *Days of Our Lives*.

I sat up and crossed my legs and breathed in deep. 'I've already told you. That first day I asked him why he was mad, and he shrugged. The next time I asked him, he raised his eyebrows. It got even more awkward after that. Eventually, I just gave up.'

'Please watch more Oprah,' Alexis said, with the conviction of an old, wise soul. She swung her legs off the bed and gripped the side of the bedframe. 'I have Dessa record it on the days we're home late from practice and I've learned a lot. I mean . . . a ton. Sometimes people don't know why things go sour. Happens all the time. That's why it's called com-mun-i-ca-tion.' She enunciated like I was thick-skulled. 'You have to open your mouth and keep asking if you want answers.'

Alexis's sister, Dessa, was twelve years older.

She was always hooking Alexis up and putting her on to grown folks' things.

A second later, Alexis suddenly shot up from the bed with her forefinger pointed in the air and shouted, '*Booyaka! Booyaka!*' while busting out the bogle, which was such a Luce move. I laughed so hard my sides stitched up and was glad she was finally doing her job. Especially since being silly wasn't Alexis's strong suit.

Now, I was ready to get back to business.

'What can I do with the space in the middle of the room, anyway?' I asked, standing up. I started pacing in front of my desk.

'I don't know, but you better make up your mind. We're running out of time. What time is Auntie's flight coming in tomorrow?'

'Late.' I grabbed the stack of papers that was sitting on top of my desk and started fanning my face. I'd been scribbling down a few words here and there for our winning chant, but I was careful to shield my handwriting from Alexis. She'd be over-the-top excited expecting to see something good and all I had was a lot of bad. 'It's something crazy, like midnight, which means I'll be asleep by the time they get here. I guess I'll see her on Monday morning.'

Alexis shrugged.

I peeled through the papers to make sure I hadn't accidentally mixed in my homework, folded the chant sheets in half, and shoved them in the top drawer just in case Aunt Rose was a snoop.

'Your momma said Auntie Rose is young, didn't she?' Alexis grinned. 'Maybe you'll be homegirls and she'll braid your hair in all the cool Tanzanian styles.'

'What makes you think they're cool?' I said, scanning my room for anything else I had to secret away from Aunt Rose.

Alexis raised an eyebrow. 'Motherland gotta be cool. *Wait?* Maybe she'll even have make-up!'

None of us wore make-up. I had no idea what crazy train Alexis was on now.

'I'm not worried about my face,' I said, grabbing a pillow from my bed. 'I'm worried about her driving me crazy, like Baba, thinking she can tell me what to do, being super nosy, and not letting me finish the chant. You know I need peace and quiet to write, and you're the one who said all aunties are nosy and loud.'

Alexis nodded slowly, crossing her arms across her chest and conjuring up wise woman again. 'True. In my experience, they are. And trust me, I feel your pain times two. Sharing a room with my cousins when they first came from Barbados drove me so far up the wall. Remember?'

I gave her a small smile. 'How could I forget? They destroyed the life out of all your stuff, including the kaleidoscope we both made. That's what I'm trying to tell you. Aunt Rose coming here is bringing major chaos to my cosmos.'

Alexis burst out laughing. 'Major *what* to your *what*?'

'You heard me.'

'We've all had relatives visit, Kam. It's not that big of a deal.'

'Forget it,' I said, knowing Alexis was really trying but would never fully understand my pain. She'd lived her whole life with family around. I hadn't. And she wasn't the one who had gotten everyone's hopes up with the idea of a winning chant. That was all me. I made a face at her. 'Just move. Let's turn the bed in the other direction.'

'*Kaaammmm!*' a voice bellowed from outside my bedroom door.

Classic Momma struck again. She always had the worst timing.

I threw my pillow at Alexis and sighed deep before stomping away.

It had to be near midnight when I realized I was still tossing and turning.

Alexis's snoring didn't help, especially since she sounded like a lawnmower.

Which made it even harder to doze off.

Since I couldn't sleep, I decided to focus on winning.

Well . . . the chant.

I had to get it right, and two weeks wasn't a lot of time to crank it out.

And practise it.

And then perfect it.

Two weeks wasn't a lot of time before our last two meets together.

The four of us had been running for three years straight. Finding our footing and freedom and, most of all, cementing our friendship. Winning the relay was the perfect way to send Luce off to her new life.

It was the right way to celebrate our foursome.

It was the only way.

It was everything.

Which brought me right back to the chant.

I knew the pressure was on when Alexis – who loved

running but mostly cared about keeping her straight As and having a constant supply of Parmesan cheese – was dropping hints about it. I turned to my side and tried to replace the sound of her racket with some of the songs I'd been listening to these days. I was hoping that maybe the big bounce of Kris Kross's 'Jump' or the deep-down groove of Pete Rock & CL Smooth's 'They Reminisce Over You' could help me work my way into something. I even went back to the bad boogie of 'You Gots to Chill' by EPMD, but nothing was catching. I had the pieces of what I wanted to say in my head, but I still couldn't fit them together.

And, of course, I couldn't help thinking of Odie.

Listening to music was our thing.

We used to get together on the last Thursday of the month, no matter what, to listen to our new CDs. I was so tired of thinking about all the things we 'used to' do.

I flopped to my other side.

Just as another tune started to worm its way around in my head, a long *pffffffffft* echoed across the room. I thought about throwing my pillow at Alexis's head, then decided that would be wrong.

Instead, I flipped and flopped some more before I eventually gave up.

My mind was on a one-way street . . . tracing its way back to February.

When everything between Odie and me fell off the track.

10.
LUNCH

'Over here,' Alexis had shouted that cold winter day. As soon as I walked through the lunchroom doors with my crinkly brown paper bag, she shot over to me, a half-eaten pear in her hand, and pulled my wrist.

Usually, I would've been with Odie.

We'd swing through the orange lunch doors together, move down the lunch line while he grabbed whatever they had: spaghetti and meatballs, or meatloaf, or grilled cheese. He'd always get a carton of milk for himself and an oatmeal raisin cookie for me. We'd plop ourselves outside on the grass and talk with our mouths full while we compared notes: *Was Mr Tierney really dozing during art class? Why would he expect us to stay awake, then? Have you heard that TLC song yet? Pretty sure it's gonna be a jam.*

When it was warm, we'd pick up the remains of our lunch extra slow and mosey on back inside the building. In winter, we'd talk fast through chattering teeth, then run inside to spend the rest of lunch period in the lounge warming up and watching the chess team battle it out in a corner.

Swishing and clomping and plopping and munching.

Hee-hawing.

The sound of us eating lunch.

Except, not that Monday.

Odie and Aunt Darien were spending the week in Nevada, which meant I was flying solo. But Alexis was dead set on my eating with her and Neeka. I could tell by the way she cleared space for me on the table and gave the evil eye to two fifth graders who had approached – and then retreated – with trays in tow.

'Where else you going?' Neeka said, looking up from the table, her mouth filled with meatball sauce.

I shrugged. 'Don't we see each other enough?'

'What on God's green earth are you talking about?' Alexis said, reaching into her lunch sack. She pulled out the main event. A pulled pork sandwich.

I pushed Neeka's tray over more. 'I don't know. All day in class. After school at track.'

Plus, I'd only ever eaten with Odie.

It was another one of the things we always did together.

Like walking to school and playing CDs.

Our steady routine.

Neeka, who was sitting on the same side of the table as me, turned her head slowly. 'Just admit it.' She grinned, using her tongue to catch some rogue meatball sauce that was about to fall off her lips.

'What?' I asked, lifting my shoulders. I pulled the apple out of my paper bag.

'You crushing on Odie, that's what,' she said. 'Anyone with eyes can see it.' She lifted her fork to her mouth and took another big bite of the meatball she'd been working on.

'I'm not crushing on anyone,' I said. I could feel hot streaks rise up my neck all the way to my face. 'Odie is my—'

'Right,' Neeka said, chopping off the rest of my words. She put her fork down and sucked up the last of her juice box. 'Your best friend. Your homey. Your blah, blah, blah.'

Alexis wiped the sides of her mouth with her napkin and started folding it into a perfect square. The only thing left of the pulled pork sandwich she'd scarfed down was the lingering smell of barbecue. 'I can't believe you,' she said, ignoring Neeka. 'You seriously don't want to eat with us? I can understand why you wouldn't want to eat with messy-mouth Neeka over there. But *me*?' She dragged the last word out.

'That's not it,' I said. 'I'd just rather eat outside and not be invaded by so much . . .' I sniffed, 'bad aroma. The food smells like vomit in here. Not yours of course.' I gave a smile. 'And Luce eats with her cousins, right?'

Alexis glared at me. 'Whatever. I just saved your tired butt from pacing around here looking like a moron.' She started gathering her trash. 'And you better eat quick. Bell's gonna ring. Then you'll really be out here on your own.' She lifted an eyebrow. 'You're welcome.'

I scrunched my face and took a massive bite of my apple.

She rolled her eyes at me. 'Lord. You stay rigid, Kam.'

Turns out, I didn't stay rigid.

I didn't get sick of them either.

I even got used to the noxious lunchroom smells.

When Odie was back at school a week later, we met up for lunch in our usual spot outside the lunchroom doors. 'You go ahead,' he said, when I asked him if he wanted to sit with me and the girls.

'You sure?' I asked, bouncing on the balls of my feet.

'Yup,' Odie said, nodding his hair back and giving me a weird, plasticky smile. 'I'm good.' He walked away and disappeared through the doors just as I was about to tell him that I'd changed my mind and we could do our usual thing.

Before I knew it, what started in February had turned into March and then April.

And us not eating lunch turned into us not hanging out any more.

Turned into light years between us.

My body flinched under the covers remembering that day all over again

I sat up in bed and looked over at Alexis.

She was still snoring like a choo-choo train.

There was no way I was coming up with anything good for the chant tonight.

I lay back down, closed my eyes, and tried to think about nothing.

11.
OUCH

On Sunday morning, after Alexis left, I finished clearing out my closet and curled up on my bed to work on the chant. Alexis had tried to pump me up before she went back home, cheering me on and saying that I would definitely write something that would send us soaring to first place. She was sure of it. But once I sat down with a pencil in one hand and a pad of paper on my knees, nothing sounded right.

I tried to match words to the rhythm in my head, but it all came out uneven.

Finding rhythm had always been a breeze.

I barely had to think about it.

I wasn't Alexis, who needed to practise the whole night to learn a simple dance step. And she could barely bust a beat.

But nothing I came up with now was smooth enough.

Everything screeched.

My flow was tapped out from all the distractions.

Disappearing best friends.

Magically appearing relatives.

Eventually, I must've dozed off because the next thing I knew Momma was shaking me awake and telling me Dacia was downstairs.

Dacia was my next-door-neighbour-hairdresser-but-really-babysitter-in-disguise.

She always came over to 'braid my hair' while Momma and Baba went out.

Usually, I made a big stink about being left behind, but this time it was working in my favour. Tomorrow was a school day, and since Aunt Rose's flight came in at 11:55 tonight, I was excused from having to head to the airport a hundred hours early to welcome her.

For once, I was grateful to be left at home.

Dacia worked at bullet-fast speed, the click-clacking of her Lee Press on Nails moving over my head in their own quick rhythm.

And every yank of my head felt like a yank into my pathetic reality:

I had barely started the chant and it was already stuck.

Ouch.

My friendship with Odie was in the dumps.

Ouch.

And I was about to be trapped in a room with Aunt Rose.

Ouch.

Dacia was yanking so hard, but every time I said, 'ouch' she said, 'what are you complaining about little girl?' and tapped the pick on my head.

I got the hint and turned my voice off, but mouthed the words to myself.

When Dacia was done with her yanking and my hairline was pulled as tight as a tied rope, I tried to scooch over and scan the pages of the romance novel she left on the floor, but like always she snatched it up and said, 'Homey, don't play that.' She bopped the book on top of my head. Then she cackled off to the kitchen to make her microwave popcorn dinner, while I pressed my fingers to my sore edges, hoping they were still there.

Clicking and clacking and ouching and cackling.

The sound of Dacia braiding my hair.

And the sound of reality *really* sinking in.

By the time Momma and Baba came back from the airport, my freshly braided head of hair and I were fast asleep. I had one more night to avoid Aunt Rose. Not that it mattered. My reality was still my reality.

Odie was still mad.

Aunt Rose was still coming.

The chant was still nothing.

And winning was still everything.

12.
GONE

I woke up on Monday morning in a puddle of light. I took the pillow off my head and turned to my side, snaking closer to the edge of the bed. It took a minute, but I eventually cracked one eye open. A long hump stretched along the spare bed, rising and falling with each silent breath. At the top of the hump, a brightly patterned headscarf stuck out of the comforter.

I couldn't see a face.

I quickly scanned the room.

A huge brown suitcase, two plastic bags doubled-up, and a black leather purse were lined up on the floor next to the bed. A Bible sat on the nightstand and what looked like a dress was folded neatly on top of my desk.

It was brightly coloured too.

What was that scent?

The room smelled sweet, like Luce's candy-coated pockets or maple syrup.

I took a deep breath.

Aunt Rose was really here.

Even though we'd slept in the same room, I still hadn't seen her.

Now, it was time to face the music.

I threw the covers off and gingerly swung my legs over the bed.

I waited a sec to see if Aunt Rose would move, but nothing.

I tiptoed to my closet, grabbed my school clothes, and snuck out to the bathroom like a cat burglar.

'There she is,' Momma said in a honeyed voice, when I rumbled into the kitchen with my backpack around both my shoulders. She was standing at the counter pouring herself a cup of tea. She bounced the tea bag up and down a few times before she pulled it out and set it on a saucer. As I swept past her, she planted a kiss on my forehead then settled at the kitchen table. 'Was your aunt awake?'

I quickly went to grab a bowl. 'Nope.' I scooped myself some oatmeal from the big red pot. I dropped the ladle, leaving a messy trail of goop on the stovetop. 'She was stone-still.' I eyed the table. Everything I needed was already there: a glass of orange juice, cinnamon, blueberries and brown sugar. I noticed it was set for four, instead of three, and my stomach roiled for a split second.

Keeping my bag on my shoulders, I sat down on the edge of my chair, threw toppings onto my steaming bowl, and scarfed down my oatmeal.

Momma picked up her mug and warmed her hands

against it. 'Makes sense she's still sleeping. We got in very late last night . . . actually, it was very early this morning when you think about it. Anyway, she is so excited to see you. And I can't wait for you to meet her. I have a feeling the two of you will—'

I shot out of my chair so quickly the screech on the wooden floor chopped off Momma's words. 'I'm sure she is and I'm sure we will. But I have to get to school because Alexis and the girls and I . . .' I took a long swig of orange juice and slammed the glass down. As I dashed to the door, I heard movement above our heads.

My feet crashed to a dead stop.

There were footsteps.

And maybe a suitcase being dragged.

'Later, Momma. The girls and I have stuff to discuss.' Which was true.

Our chant was still not finished.

It was barely started.

Everything was at stake.

Momma stood up. 'Wait, Kam. What's the rush? I think your aunt is awake. Maybe you can just say a quick hello before you—'

But since talking in the morning wasn't my thing, I wasn't friends with change and Aunt Rose was *already* messing up my flow, I didn't wait for Momma to finish.

I was already gone.

13.
FOCUS
AND CONTROL

School went by in a daze. I wasn't sure if it was because I had been focusing so hard on the chant, or because hearing Odie laugh out loud in third period science class pricked my heart, or because I was about to meet Aunt Rose.

Even practice was a blur.

On our way home, the girls and I stopped at the Wawa convenience store a few blocks from school. Evening traffic whizzed by outside the glass door.

A siren wailed in the distance.

Alexis waved me over to the magazine rack while she munched on a bag of corn chips. 'Look,' she said, pointing at one of our favourite groups on the cover of a music magazine. Her mouth was full. Corn chip pieces fell to the floor. 'They look so cute.'

Her eyes shifted down to my hands. 'You, on the

other hand, with your Cheese Curls and your orange fingers. Not cute. I don't know how you can eat something orange that's not, you know, an orange.' She shook her head like I'd committed the original sin.

I raised my eyebrow. High. 'But you drink orange soda.'

Alexis made a face. 'Not the same thing. *Obviously*.'

Alexis was like this. A wiz until she wasn't. I don't know where her good sense went, but it wasn't in the Wawa with us. I pulled a Cheese Curl out of the bag, held it up with two fingers, popped it in my mouth, and crunched it in her face, Luce-like.

Orange cheese dust floated to the floor.

Micky, who worked the cash register, let us eat like this before we paid because she always said, 'I know all that looping in circles around that track makes you girls hangry.'

Luce skip-walked over to us from the candy aisle. 'Don't sleep on the sugar. *Pah-pow!*' Her hands were heavy with the whole sugar rainbow.

Skittles, Starbursts, Now & Laters and her favourite, Bazooka bubble gum.

'Come on, guys,' Neeka said, joining us. 'It's getting late. Besides, Kam has to meet Auntie.' She shimmied her legs while pulling up her black sweats for the hundredth time because even though she was size S, she always wore size L. 'By the way, where we at with the words for our big win?'

She rubbed her hands together like she was waiting for the tastiest treat.

Even her eyes got sparkly.

I fidgeted with my almost empty bag of Cheese Curls. 'You mean the chant?'

'No,' Neeka said, grinning. 'The words written across your forehead. Of course, the chant.' Her hips got loose and her legs started whirling like she was ready to start practising on the spot.

Luce's little legs started up, too. She did a jig right there, slapping her treasure trove together in her hands while she danced, the plastic wrapping crinkling and crackling and popping, while she stomped to her candy beat. 'I know you got it, Kam.' Clap. 'Spill a bean.' Clap. 'Say a word.' Clap. 'What, what!' Clap.

Clapping and stomping and clapping and stomping.

The sound of a whole bunch of pressure.

Luce took a breath and said, 'We're about to be unstoppable!'

I made a sour face.

Luce stopped dancing. She traded glances with Alexis and Neeka. '*What?*'

'The words haven't been exactly flowing,' I said.

'Well, do you need some help?' Neeka asked, her voice reaching out softer than usual, which only made me feel worse. 'We all know I'm no good with words. But heck if I can't help you bend that beat.'

I stayed quiet.

Alexis pulled me by the sleeve of my windbreaker to the cash register. 'Is it the whole Aunt Rose thing? Or Odie?'

'Odie,' Neeka piped up from behind us.

I could hear Luce smacking her with her candy stash.

Alexis looped her arm around my shoulder. 'I just watched an episode of Oprah. She was talking about the phone call as an expression of love. Pick up the phone, Kam, and call Odie.'

'*Ewww*,' Luce said, flanking my other side. 'What's love got to do with it?'

I rolled my eyes and sighed.

'Don't worry,' Luce said. She dropped her candy on the counter and grinned widely at Micky. Micky grinned back and started ringing her up. Luce turned back to me. 'Alexis is just being disgusting. Back to the chant, you have a way with words. It's gonna be dope. And we're gonna be the flyest seventh graders to ever win the 4 x 100 relay. Case closed.'

I tipped my head back and dumped the last of the Cheese Curls into my mouth.

If only.

I handed the bag over to Micky, who scanned it and then tossed it in the trash.

I slapped a dollar on the counter and she took it.

Neeka turned me around by the shoulders to face her. 'You know I'm the first one to pop your bubble if I feel you're blowing yourself up too big. But we all know you can do this. Words are your speciality. Just think about it this way. We've come so close to winning so many times. Like you always shout, we've had so many second places! But you know what's different this time around?' Neeka paused. I kept quiet. She barrelled on. 'We've never had a chant to really bring it all together. Your words plus our flow for our last race together equals first place, baby! And just like running a race, you have to find that focus and control. Then you got it. Don't worry about Aunt Rose or your boyfriend . . . um, I mean Odie.' Then Neeka did the unexpected. She gave me a big smile, which was kind of freaky and definitely made me wonder if this was a body double and the real naysaying Neeka was at home.

Micky interrupted to tell us to move back and make way for other paying customers and the girls pulled me aside and crowded around me, slugging me in the arm to hype me up.

I let a smile slip out, then felt a small piece of me sink when they all smiled back.

Even though this was how it was supposed to be.

We always rallied around each other when one of us needed help.

We always found comfort and cheer in our flow.

Writing something that could bring us together, so we could win together, would feel like this, but a million times better.

Right now, the girls were doing their part, gassing me up.

I just hoped I could do mine.

14.
IN THE FLESH

She wore a smile that stretched from one side of her face all the way to the other. And even before I crossed the threshold of the kitchen, she jumped up and ran over to me like we were long-lost best friends.

Aunt Rose was here all right.

In the flesh.

And I quickly got the sense that we didn't feel the same way about personal space.

Or slowly getting to know one another.

'*Njoo*. Come,' she squealed, pulling me in so tight she nearly squeezed all the air out of my lungs. I almost choked, but she kept on gripping me and squealing and rocking me from side to side like I was a rag doll. After a few seconds of whiplash, I was released from the death grip. But Aunt Rose held on to my shoulders while she looked me over.

'*Eh hehn!*' she said like Baba always did, only in a much softer voice.

She twisted me from side to side over and over again.

I could finally get a better look at her, too. The skin on her face was dark and velvety smooth. Her teeth, pearly white like Baba's. They practically lit up the entire room. She was the same frame as all the other Kessy women I'd seen in pictures.

Tall and slim.

I recognized the sharp cheek bones too. She wore a pink house dress with lots of different coloured dots. Tiny micro braids were rolled into a neat bun on top of her head. Before she let me go, she held my arms out wide. 'You're getting so tall. You'll be taller than me soon. Maybe tall like Baba.'

I stared at her thick, curly eyelashes for a second before I decided I couldn't hold the comment against her. How could she know that the thought of being tall made me miserable?

I organized my face into a smile and tried to resist the urge to bolt.

The whole time, Aunt Rose kept hold of my hands.

'Oh, don't be shy,' she bellowed. 'Sing! Dance! We are finally together!'

We? Finally?

I tried to let go of her but she wasn't having it so I let her lead me to the table. I sat down matter-of-factly while she took her seat as bright as any sun I'd ever seen.

I sighed deep on the inside.

Momma rose to her feet, her blue eyes sparkling. 'Look at you two! We need pictures!' I'd barely noticed

Baba, who was sitting at the kitchen table still in his work clothes. While Momma dashed off to grab the camera, Baba beamed at me with a smile a mile wide.

'Well look at us,' he said, turning his eyes to Aunt Rose then back to me. 'Three Kessys around the table. *Mungu ni mwema.*'

God is good. The one Kiswahili phrase I knew.

A breeze came in from the window behind Baba and I recognized Dacia's theatrical voice cutting through the air.

'First thing is the first,' Aunt Rose said, breaking the silence and remixing the expression. 'I have a few rituals. You know, things to help make a home happy. Tell me what you like to eat, Kamaria, and I will cook it. Anything, anything.' She leaned over and squeezed my hand. 'The juiciest most delicious anything.'

My ears might have involuntarily perked up for a sec when Aunt Rose said the word ritual. I knew how important those were.

But I didn't like forced bonding.

And I didn't want to be force-fed Tanzanian food.

So, I just cracked a tiny smile and shrugged and hoped, for my sake, that the rest of my good manners showed up soon.

15.
SLOW TO WARM

'I know you,' Aunt Rose said later that night. 'You are slow to warm.' Her voice lulled in that Swahili way I'd only gotten glimpses of when Baba was around other Tanzanians.

Slow to warm.

The words hung between us as we got ready for bed for the first time together.

I shrugged out of my robe, keeping a straight face.

I figured if she caught on that she was right about that one thing, she might be convinced that she knew me for real.

I was dead sure she didn't.

I slid off my pink slippers and climbed into bed, still creeped out about sleeping next to someone I barely knew.

Aunt Rose, still as chipper as ever, made herself right at home.

She picked up a jar of Vaseline, which looked

suspiciously like mine. She opened it and dug out a fingerful. Then she smeared it on her smooth arms in big strokes. 'I know you are like this because it's the Kessy way,' she said after some time had passed. She closed the jar and plopped it back on the side table. Then she fished around in her plastic toiletry case looking for something. The roses on the plastic case were faded to brown, like she'd crisscrossed the world with it.

Which she hadn't. Coming here was the first time she'd ever set foot on a plane.

A few more long moments passed before she said with a smirk. 'I am the opposite of slow to warm. I warm up fast, fast.'

She could say that again.

While Aunt Rose settled into bed, I was deciding if I was going to retrieve my jar of Vaseline or just let her have it now that she'd literally left her mark on it.

She hadn't even asked me if she could use it.

A second later I realized it didn't matter. I couldn't let Aunt Rose's being here break my focus.

Only one thing really mattered in the next twelve days.

The thing looping around my head like a broken record.

Write. Run. Win.

16.
RHYTHM ON
MY MIND

On the walk to school the next morning, the sky swirled with dark clouds that were no match for my bad mood.

The clock was ticking. We needed the chant in less than two weeks.

I'd talked a big game about writing something.

Something that sounded like us. Something that could get us hyped up.

Something to send us shooting like stars straight into first place.

It was easy.

Write. Run. Win.

Just a few days ago, I knew I could do it. Now here I was drawing blanks, worrying that I wouldn't be able to close the deal.

The wind picked up and everything whirred around me in a rhythmless rumble – from the heavy clouds up above to the trash circling aimlessly at my feet. I cut across the street towards the back-alley shortcut that Odie and I used to take on the way to school, which only made me wish he was right here with me.

Focus, Kam.

I had to focus. I had to keep rhythm on my mind.

Write. Run. Win.

I continued walking, hefting my backpack on my shoulder. It wasn't long before another thing started creeping into my head. Something Aunt Rose had said just before she conked out last night. She said she usually sang old Kiswahili songs before bed. They had a special rhythm that were good for sleeping. Thank God she didn't sing one. But that was only because right after the words came out of her mouth, she was fast asleep. I looked at her a little surprised. Not because she'd shut her eyes faster than a blink, but because she'd been talking about rhythm. Earlier that night, she'd mentioned rituals. Rhythm and rituals.

I guess paying attention to these things ran in the family.

I stepped off the concrete kerb, pushed Aunt Rose *way* out of my head, and returned to the chant.

I thought about the sound of feet hitting the track.

I shook my head.

What about the click-crack of the starting gun?

Little Luce swooping around the curve?

What sound did that make exactly?

Alexis flying over a hurdle?

Neeka's Nike running shorts?

They swished, right?

The roar of the stands?

Nope.

Maybe I needed to focus on words instead of sounds.

I thought about Jody Watley crooning about friends.

That was definitely us!

Then there was the song Alexis loved by Luther and Janet that just came out.

What were they singing about?

Something about the best things in life being free . . .

Running was free.

Nope. Not good.

Bad.

Very bad.

I switched gears again.

Maybe I needed something fresh like 'It Takes Two' by Rob Base and DJ E-Z Rock.

Maybe we shouldn't have clowned Luce after all.

Maybe she was right.

Maybe hip-hop was gonna be the magic spot.

I whispered two lines of the song to myself before I realized it was just another bad idea. Odie and I always listened to this song when we were prepping for exams.

Who would I be prepping with for final exams now?

Not Odie.

Focus and control, Kam. Focus on the chant. Focus on winning!

Especially since we were already losing.

We were going to lose Luce, so losing the race was not an option!

Suddenly, I heard a titanic roar.

Then beeping, banging and clanging.

The sound of the garbage truck nearly knocked me off my feet, sending everything I had, which amounted to a whole bunch of nothing, out of my head.

Here I was again.

At another dead end.

PART TWO:
GET SET

17.
T MINUS
TEN DAYS

'What's the torture today?' Luce asked on the way to practice on Wednesday.

It was championship season. That meant Coach Rosse didn't play.

'Definitely hills,' Alexis said.

Luce sighed dramatically. *'Not again!'*

'All part of winning,' I said, very matter of fact.

Neeka nodded her agreement.

The sun peeked from behind a cloud and started beating down on our heads as we dragged our slow bones past a row of old ash trees with furrowed bark. On the asphalt path to our right, overzealous people roller-bladed and biked on by. Ahead of us, Coach fuzzed in and out of focus as he paced on top of Gravity Hill. We called it that because whether you went up or down, it felt like gravity was working hard against you. We were still moving as slow as molasses when we heard Coach shout, 'Evans, Kessy, Vidal, Davenport!' Then he charged down the hill and started rounding up the rest of the team, tapping his clipboard to make the point.

But nobody was late. Coach hadn't blown his whistle yet. That happened at 3 p.m. on the dot. Coach was pretty serious about his 'three strikes' rule, too.

You could be late once. That was the freebie.

If you were late twice, you couldn't run in the next meet.

If you were late three times, good luck.

You'd have to find another team, because you weren't staying on his. Coach wasn't *mean* mean. He always kept a smile tucked away deep in his back pocket for when you did good. Or for when he dared you to quit.

Just like Baba.

But when he meant business, he meant business.

That was like Baba too.

'Speaking of winning,' Luce said as we got closer to the patchy grassy area at the bottom of the hill where the rest of the girls' track team was straggling in. She looked at me and gave me a soft nudge. 'How's it going?'

I wiped some sweat off my brow and shrugged.

I was still at a dead end, going absolutely nowhere fast.

I still couldn't seem to find my groove.

But I couldn't tell that to the girls.

Luce grabbed my arm and smiled wide. 'Don't worry. It's coming. You got this.'

Neeka turned to me. 'You know when I told Dama you were coming up with a little something she got all excited. She said back when she ran in the state meet her team got together and belted out 'Shake Your Thang' by Salt-N-Pepa beforehand. And as you know, the rest was history. I told her she better go sit down with her Salt-N-Pepa butt because we would be winning on a Kam Kessy *o-ri-gi-nal*!'

Damayanti was Neeka's big sister. She was a track superstar. And Lisa Bonet cool.

She was basically everything we ever dreamed of and more. The thought of her knowing I was working on a chant made me sick to my stomach.

'Don't pressure her!' Alexis said. She gave me a kind smile.

'That's not pressure,' Neeka said. 'That's gas. Just some fuel for the tank.'

'For the genius,' Luce added, elbowing me and grinning like Bozo the Clown.

'Wait?' Alexis said, smirking. 'So ... like ... now Kam's all that and a bag of chips and she hasn't even shared a word? How's that look?'

I swung my leg out and Alexis dodged my kick, clinging onto Neeka's arm.

Luce dug into her pockets. 'Look,' she said, holding up a small, crinkled bag of barbeque chips. 'I got a bag, too.' She stuck her fingers in and licked the salty crumbs.

'Gross,' Neeka said.

'What?' Luce said, shrugging her shoulders. She

71

turned around to face me and started walking backwards. '*Soooo*, what's Auntie Rose been cooking?'

I smiled, more than relieved to move on from the chant. 'The works. And she's only been here three days. She made these sweet-cinnamony donuts called *mandazi* from scratch. I can't lie. They were so good.'

Luce rubbed her tummy. Her eyes were hungry.

'And then this spicy beef stew. Grilled red snapper. I mean it's like . . .'

'Hog heaven . . .' Luce finished, licking her lips.

I chuckled. 'I was gonna say gourmet. She sings while she cooks, too.'

Luce laughed. 'Now that's my kind of Auntie. When Tía Domi comes to visit us, she brings all the sunshine from Puerto Rico with her. She sings and twirls nonstop like she's Rita Moreno. She cooks all day too. Pasteles. Mofongo. Mamí says she's where I get my battery from. And why I talk a mile a minute. She says every last bit of me is her sister.'

Alexis laughed. 'I met Tía Domi that one time, 'member? You *are* her carbon copy. She's even tiny like you.'

'Momma keeps saying I look like Aunt Rose,' I said, shuffling my feet as I walked.

'Looking like family is the best,' Neeka chimed. 'I favour my daddy's side too. Most of my aunties have calves like me. They call them the Davenport calves. Made for quickness. And at least two of my aunties have green eyes. Every year at the family reunion in Louisiana,

72

Daddy's there, sitting round the table with them, discussing family business. And, bam, outta nowhere: 'You three are the only ones in the whole history of this family that have those ocean eyes.' Like Daddy even knows the whole history of the family. We must've gotten 'em from somewhere. Anyway, having a family likeness is how you know you belong to something. Which is dope.'

I just nodded silently and listened while they kept on talking.

I half understood what Neeka meant. A lot of the expressions Aunt Rose used were just like Baba's. And last night, Aunt Rose told me a little bit about her home in Dar es Salaam. Which reminded me of Baba too. But her story was a million times better than anything Baba ever shared.

It was song-like.

Not that I let Aunt Rose know that. I just nodded and smiled small. I guess I was torn.

On the one hand, I *was* a little more curious about Aunt Rose.

On the other, I was still aggravated.

Both days after school this week, I'd found her snoozing in the bedroom. Momma called it jet lag.

I called it cramping my style. She made it impossible for me to be alone in my room with my inspiration:

My track posters and awards.

The magazine cover with Flo-Jo.

And the Olympic rings on my ceiling.

This is where things always came together in my head.

It's where I had been playing the win in my mind for a whole year.

It's where I needed to write.

The girls tried to help when they told me, 'We've all *been* shared a room, Kam.'

But they didn't get it.

Only Odie would truly feel my pain. He didn't have siblings, just like me. He didn't grow up around other family either. He got why I was slow to warm. And why sharing a room was trying my patience and hijacking my focus.

No privacy. No peace.

My steps grew heavy the more I thought about it.

If I could talk to Odie right now, he'd find a way to get me to see past Aunt Rose.

To clear away all the noise in my head and write.

And if I could write the chant, I could close the deal.

We would win.

I only had ten more days . . .

A second later, Alexis was tugging on my arm. 'Let's stop lollygagging and hurry up,' she said. 'Coach is looking kinda heated.'

18.
AN ADJUSTMENT

'Thank you for joining us, ladies,' Coach said when we finally sat down on the grass. I swiped my knees back and forth like windshield wipers and looked at my watch.

2:58 p.m.

We were the last ones to sit down, but we were still on time.

Coach turned to stand in front of the whole group and a minute later, he blew his whistle. Right on cue, the preaching began.

'OK, now listen up, warriors. It's Wednesday. We only have a week and a half of practices left before regionals, which you know is a week on Saturday. And with some good effort, I know we have a shot at winning first place in the team competition this year. *Do you hear me?*'

Coach leaned over to the right, bending his knee like he was about to take off sideways. He cupped his hand around his ear to catch our response.

'*We hear you!*' the entire team shouted back with excitement.

'And winning starts now, not at the meet. *Are we together?*' Coach straightened up and spread his arms out wide like an eagle.

'*We're together!*' we shouted back.

'OK. Questions?' Coach slowly walked around the grass before planting his feet back in front of the team. He cocked his hat to the side. Which meant sermon over.

Luce and I grinned at each other. Coach's hat looked about a hundred years old. And it was always *almost* falling off. It was threatening to fall off completely now, but by some miracle it stayed glued to his head. Luce elbowed me in the ribs to make sure I was still watching. I poked her back and tried to wrestle the smile from my lips.

Neeka raised her hand. Coach gave a nod. 'Are you sure who's running in the 4 x 100 relay at the regional meet?' she asked, emphasizing the 'you sure' part. 'No switch-ups?'

His eyes tightened. 'Neeka, you can expect to be running with Kam, Alexis and Luce. But as you know, I may have to make an adjustment to the line-up at the last—'

'*An adjustment?*' Neeka sassed back before Coach could finish.

Her eyes stretched wide.

I stiffened.

Neeka had just broken Coach's cardinal rule: When Coach talks, you listen.

I peeked over at the girls.

Luce was chewing on her fingernails.

Alexis was fiddling with her shoelaces.

I knew better than to make direct eye contact with either of them.

If Coach caught us trading sly glances or hushed words, we could all be sidelined on Saturday at the regional meet. Maybe even at the state meet.

Coach pressed his lips together. 'Neeka, we'll talk after practice. *Understand?*'

Neeka nodded reluctantly.

My stomach dropped.

19.
WE RUN
WE WIN

Momma was big on clearing out bad energy. She had her own ways to do it – waving crystals, spraying special water and other mysterious things. Energy cleansing is what she called it. And after that outburst from Neeka, we had some bad energy clearing of our own to do.

Alexis and I stared at each other to see who was going to go first.

First one to blink lost. That was me.

I turned to face Neeka and took a deep breath. 'Why'd you have to go and get Coach all cranked? You know his rule is—'

She blinked, cutting me off with her eyes before her mouth even opened. 'Why are you always trying to put things that aren't crooked straight? He asked if there were any questions, *right*?'

'I guess,' I said, raising my hands and clasping them

78

behind my head. I braced myself. 'But you know he'll be quick to pull you. Then all of us lose.'

'Trust me,' Neeka said. 'I'm doing this for us. Coach isn't always right just because he's Coach. We have parents. We know how wrong adults can be.'

I watched Alexis turning Neeka's words over in her head like they just might hold some secret wisdom. After a second, she shook her head dubiously.

I guess she decided Neeka was wrong.

'All I'm saying is that the extra hard work we put in better not be in vain,' Neeka continued.

'*Or what?*' Alexis said, shifting her stance. 'What are you gonna do? Bum rush the track?'

'It's simple,' I said to Neeka. 'We run. We win.'

She threw me a look. 'Exactly. We're letting you do your part, right? Let me do mine. You focus on the writing, let me focus on the line up.'

I blinked. Neeka had a point.

Even if I was getting nowhere, we each had our own roles to play. 'Um, OK,' I said knowing what I wanted to say but not daring to say it, which was my chant could only help us win if we were all on the track.

Unlike last year . . .

20.
DEAL?

Last year, our relay team was good. Really good. Our race times told us so. And we knew we had a fighting chance to win the regional championship.

Maybe the state championship, too.

But on the bus ride to the regional meet, Neeka made a smart remark about Coach. He heard her. And it didn't go down easy.

Coach switched Neeka out for Esabella Rice faster than Luce scarfs down Skittles.

Esabella was fast. But she wasn't part of our rhythm and flow.

And for the 4 x 100 relay, we passed the baton blindly, which meant the runner didn't turn her head to look back for it once she started running. She faced forward with her feet flying and shot her hand back.

She had to know the baton was gonna be there.

Handoffs like that took practice.

And faith.

And flow.

Which Alexis, Neeka, Luce and I all had with one another in spades.

It didn't work the same that day, though.

We were neck and neck with Chesterfield for first place when Alexis passed off to me and I passed off to Luce. By the time Luce reached Esabella for the last leg, she had a 10-yard lead on them. And that's when things fell apart. Luce passed off to Esabella, but the handoff was botched. It's not like Esabella dropped the baton or anything – that would've been the ultimate disaster – it just took a split second too long for the pass to stick. And a split second in a lightning-fast race is more like a lifetime.

Neeka swore it was because Esabella had butter-fingers, but it was probably just a combination of her nerves and not enough practice.

Whatever it was, we got smoked. Came in fourth place.

Losing so badly was still sharp in Neeka's memory.

Mine too.

It's one of the reasons why we needed the chant to set our feet on fire.

It's one of the reasons why we *had* to win.

That and the fact that these were our last two races together as a team.

This was it. Our last shot at being forever connected.

I put my arm around Neeka's shoulder. 'Look. Let's just agree not to say or do anything stupid until the season is over. You work on keeping yourself in Coach's good graces and I'll work on something to help us fly. *Deal?*'

We started walking again to catch up to the rest of the girls. The team was still wiping grass off their shorts and stretching out their limbs as they followed Coach Rosse to Gravity Hill.

'Sounds good to me,' Luce said.

Neeka fake-sneered in her direction.

'Me too,' Alexis said.

'All right,' Neeka said, looking at me as we slipped in with the team. 'But don't ask me to speak up when we need it either.'

The green and gold in her eyes were swirling a warning sign.

My mouth dried up.

Neeka and her warnings.

She knew I was superstitious, but I swallowed and nodded and stopped myself from saying anything else.

I didn't want to jinx us.

Coach clapped his hands twice. 'OK. Let's put some work in. And remember, knees high. Hips forward. Don't get sloppy now.'

21.
NOT
ODYSSEUS CUTE

We got started quick at practice the next day under thick cloud cover and the threat of rain again. After we circled the track twice to warm up, we did a few stretches, heel steps and toe steps and walking lunges with twists.

Luce was in her silly mood and had us all cracking up during drills.

As soon as Coach turned his back, Luce stuck her arms out in front of her and pretended she was Frankenstein. She was quick, though. When he swung around to face us again, she dropped her hands and snapped back into line before he could see what she was doing.

Luce loved track.

She definitely loved to win.

But she hated practice.

That's why she clowned so much. She could only get away with her clowning during warm-up, though. The rest of practice was serious.

That meant pick-ups: sprinting as fast as we could for a hundred yards, then jogging for two hundred yards at half speed.

Six times in a row without a real break in between.

Luce looked at me after one round, panting, and said, 'At least it's not hills.'

It wasn't as hard as hills. Still, Coach Rosse *did* try to kill us.

I couldn't tell if practice was harder or I was slower, but I definitely wasn't as fast as I needed to be. I just didn't have the same focus and control thanks to everything swirling in my head.

I could only hope the girls didn't notice and the chant came quick.

At the end of practice, Luce whispered, 'You think Coach is gonna say something about me leaving?' Then she fake-cried, rubbing her eyes dramatically.

'You know Coach,' I said, yawning. I dipped my head back, stretched up on my tippy toes, and came back down.

Coach was hard core. Not sentimental.

Luce bent over now and loosened her laces. 'Well, I'ma miss you guys next year.'

'Don't remind me,' I groaned.

Groaning and moaning and huffing and puffing.

Thumping and bumping and laughing and whooping.

The sound of track, especially with Luce.

I shook off the thought of her leaving as we jogged to catch up to Alexis and Neeka.

Alexis suddenly turned to me. 'What day is it today?'

'Why are you asking me?' I answered. Alexis had the habit of treating me like I was her secretary sometimes.

'Because you always know!' she said.

I rolled my eyes. 'It's Thursday . . .' and then I looked at the date window on my watch to make sure. 'The thirtieth. And just in case you're curious. It's April.'

Alexis pushed me. 'I know the month, dummy.'

'Hmm,' she said a second later, looking confused. 'I thought today was Tuesday. My bad. I guess I'm on rugrat duty. Let's hope my nephews act human for a change.'

Suddenly, my skin went tingly as it dawned on me.

It was the last Thursday of the month.

The day Odie and I would usually meet up at my house to play CDs.

My face dropped.

'What's wrong with you now?' Neeka asked, looking squarely at me.

I glanced over at Alexis and tried to give her a pleading look so she wouldn't bring it up. I didn't want to talk about it. 'Nothing,' I said to Neeka, picking up the pace.

'Oh, I know,' said Luce, who was in the middle of being mesmerized by a pack of M&M's. Still, no matter what, she never missed a beat of drama. She dug her fingers in the bag and pulled out the last few, popping them in her mouth. 'It's her Thursday CD thingy. She made that sad puppy dog face last month, too.'

I stuffed my hands into the pockets of my sweatpants and took a deep breath.

Neeka yanked on my arm. 'Maybe if you get back together with Odysseus, or Odie or O or whatever you're calling him this year, he can help you come up with something for the chant. The clock is kind of ticking.' Her long black braid thumped against her back as she smirk-walked, pulling me with her.

Before I could say anything about the five stupid words I'd written since the last time she asked me, which was yesterday, Alexis quickly said, 'Ignore her.' She sidled up to me and wrapped her arm around my shoulder. 'She's the one with a crush on Dion Weeks.'

'*Ohmygod*,' Neeka pleaded. 'You're so tedious, Alexis. Stop saying that.'

'What? You just told me he looked like Dwayne Wayne and *ohmygod* they have the same initials and we all know how you feel about Dwayne Wayne.'

'Yup!' Luce and I chorused.

'Please,' Neeka said, looking at me sideways.

I squinted my eyes at her and cracked a smile. 'Dion is cute.'

We reached the locker rooms.

Neeka tried to wipe the smile from her face but it was a lost cause. 'True. But he's not *Odysseus* cute.'

Neeka held the door open with her foot and we all scooted by. And while she swished past me, and Alexis and Luce grabbed their bags, my stomach kept turning in circles thinking about what she had just said.

Not Odysseus cute.

22.
THE LONG
WAY HOME

We finished practice early, so I decided to take the long way home. Past the school's brick walls to the corner store at the end of the street. A left turn. Three more blocks. And then a right turn onto Odie's street. I had to travel a few more blocks past Odie's house to get to mine this way, but I didn't mind. I was up for the walk. Besides, it had been two months since I'd used this route and, if I was honest, a part of me also wanted to walk past Odie's house and look up at his window.

Maybe Neeka had a point.

Maybe just being close to the old Odie energy could help with the chant.

When I turned right onto Odie's street, I stopped to check the clouds.

They were still gloomy grey and the sun was still playing hide-and-seek.

The baseball field was up ahead, and as soon as I saw it, I could feel my heartbeat change. It started booming in my chest.

I kept walking.

A few steps later, I saw Odie.

He was sitting on his stoop.

I knew there'd be a small chance I could run into him, but I wasn't expecting it.

I didn't know what to think.

Was this a stroke of good luck or a bad omen?

Every inch of me was scared stiff.

Odie must've just gotten home because his backpack was still slung over his shoulder. His hair fell like rain to his collar, hiding his eyes. Same as when we were kids. Only it was walnut-coloured now instead of white blond with a perfect side part.

My cheeks warmed as I inched forward.

Then I stopped suddenly, wondering if I should back up.

What was I going to say?

I couldn't just wing it.

I could count the number of conversations we'd had since February on one hand.

I remembered every word.

Two of them were in science class where Odie had been forced to talk to me about the end-of-year Night of Learning project by Mr Dobalina, who'd split the class into groups. The last one barely involved talking. It was when Baba took Odie and me to the dentist two weeks before Aunt Rose came. That day, when we pulled up to

Odie's brownstone, he was scowling so hard Baba had asked me what was wrong.

'Don't ask me,' I mumbled from the back seat. I sank back and watched Odie dart off the pavement and into the front seat so fast I barely saw his face. His shoulders were hitched high when he thumped down, but as soon as he pulled the seat belt over his chest and buckled in, they dropped back into their proper place.

Baba had that effect on him.

I was hoping it meant things might thaw out between us. At least for the car ride.

They didn't.

Odie mostly ignored me.

When the conversation turned to Tanzania (Classic Baba), I really wanted to escape. Instead, I clamped my eyes shut and forced myself to sit through being ignored by Odie and bored stiff by Baba telling Odie what he missed most about home.

'Maybe one day you'll visit Tanzania,' I heard Baba tell Odie at one point. 'Although your friend back there has never been too eager.' My eyes were still closed, but I rolled them anyways. A second later my heart leaped when I thought I heard Odie grumble something in response, but I must have been mistaken because the conversation switched to basketball and I went back to being bored and ignored.

I was in front of his stoop now with its black iron railing that looked just like ours. I took a sharp breath. 'Hey, Odie.'

He tilted his head in my direction and his face froze.

I could tell he was surprised. Then another look crossed over his face, but I couldn't read it. An eternity passed.

'Hey,' he said finally sweeping hair from his eyes.

A high school baseball game was on and the street was lined with cars.

Beats bumped out of a speaker somewhere.

Before, Odie and I would've just jumped right in, talking non-stop, barely taking breaths. We'd probably start with the loud cringy songs Mr Warnock had played at the rally or how Charity Evans threw up a mess of chunky hot dogs at lunch. If it had been way back when we were little, we'd be talking about the mandarin and animal crackers that were waiting for us at my house.

That was our old rhythm.

Now, nothing but silence.

I stood as still as stone, feeling foolish.

I realized I was clenching my fists and let them go.

I started climbing the steps towards him because what else was I going to do and then out of the blue, I was stunned by a sharp sound.

A kazoo buzzed.

Someone shouted, '*The Big O!*' before whizzing past us in a blur.

I stood frozen. 'Who was that?'

'It was Dennis,' Odie said. 'Didn't you see his floppy red hat fly by?'

'No,' I said, unwrapping my backpack from my shoulder and plopping myself down two stairs below him.

90

Both of us looked straight ahead at the baseball field.

After the longest forever, Odie finally said, 'So, what's up?'

I craned my neck back to face him.

His eyes were a puzzle.

I opened my mouth, but the words got stuck in my throat.

It took a second to push them out. 'Not much.'

We stayed quiet for a few awkward moments longer and went back to looking at the baseball field. In front of us, a kid took to the mound and swung his bat back.

I sucked in a lungful of air. 'Guess what?' I said, casually because I couldn't think of anything else to say. My eyes were still on the batter, who was about to strike out. 'I'm working on a chant for the regional meet next week. It's gonna be all about me and the girls coming together and winning first place.' Fiddling with the strings on my windbreaker, I turned back up to look at him

He locked eyes with me. 'Is that what you wanted to say?'

The muscles in my stomach clenched tighter than a knot.

I guessed so, but I wasn't sure. What else could I say?

To be honest, Odie, I really don't know what I did wrong.

Why can't you just tell me what I did?

The words died on the tip of my tongue.

Odie rolled his eyes. He stood up slowly, turning

away, his back hunched like he was carrying a ton of bricks.

'Forget it,' I said, standing up too.

Next thing I knew, I was grabbing my backpack and running all the way home.

23.
MIDNIGHT LESSONS

That night, the big storm finally came. The thunderclap woke me first.

I sighed as the roof rattled. I could never sleep through thunder.

Neither could Odie, although he would never admit it.

A small wave of anger started to rise up inside me thinking about the stoop.

Why couldn't Odie just spell it out and tell me what I did wrong?

A few minutes later, after I'd had enough of my pitiful self, I decided that since I was awake, I'd better make use of the time.

Who could sleep anyway?

Write. Run. Win. Write. Run. Win. Write. Run. Win.

I repeated the words in my head like a mantra, then got started piecing words and sounds together into a zinger for the girls.

Boom, boom, boom, boom.

Poom, poom, poom, poom.

Zoom, zoom, zoom, zoom.

Run, smack, fly, free. Heartbeat.

The sound of a flop.

Another thunderclap ricocheted around the room, much louder this time, and I looked over to check on Aunt Rose. She sat up quietly.

She switched on the light by her bedside table and picked up her Bible.

She read for what seemed like forever before she noticed my open eyes.

She put the Bible down in her lap. 'Kamaria, are you awake?'

'Yup,' I said, yawning.

'Can you try to read something?' she asked. 'Let me get you a book from your bookshelf.' She started to climb out of bed.

'It's OK, Aunt Rose. I'll fall back asleep. Just gonna take me a while.'

'Let me sing then.' She coughed to clear her throat, then stopped herself short. 'No. Let me tell you a story. A proper one this time. Not the small things I have been telling you here and there. This always worked for my *watoto* when they were little babies.'

'I'm fine,' I said, sounding less friendly than I wanted to because I was still annoyed at Odie, distracted by the chant, and terrified by the storm. And just because something worked for her kids, didn't mean it would work for me. I gave a small smile to make up for it, but Aunt Rose didn't seem to notice. Instead, she laughed. The laugh rang out like a crisp bell – *ting-a-ling-ling-ling* – right there in the darkness of night.

Aunt Rose settled back in her bed, and I was happy our conversation was over.

But Aunt Rose wasn't over anything. She started talking again. 'Do you know where we come from?' she asked.

I took a deep-down breath before I answered. 'You mean Tanzania?'

'I mean the place in Tanzania.'

'I have no idea, Aunt Rose.' I yawned louder this time to make the point, although I had already learned a few things about Aunt Rose. Besides having hardly any personal boundaries, she couldn't take a hint either.

'Shame on Baba!' she said. 'Let me start from the beginning . . . at the foot of Mount Kilimanjaro.' She paused for a second and raised an eyebrow. 'You do know Mount Kilimanjaro?'

I had a half second to come up with a good plan.

If I answered every question Aunt Rose threw at me, this could turn into some kind of midnight lesson and I would be up all night not making progress on the chant.

If I didn't answer any of her questions, who knew what could happen. She might report me to Momma and Baba for being rude and I'd be in more hot water than a boiling egg. I had to find the middle ground. I yawned again, overcome by true tiredness, and decided that maybe answering Aunt Rose's questions without using actual words would do the trick.

I shook my head, no, which was true.

I had *heard* of Mount Kilimanjaro. But I didn't know a single thing about it.

'That's fine,' Aunt Rose continued, rolling her body to face mine and propping her head in her hand. 'I prefer my version, anyway. I add more sweetness to the story than our other family members, including your baba.' She chuckled. 'So, Mount Kilimanjaro. Shall I continue?'

Reluctantly, I nodded yes and rubbed at my eyes.

Aunt Rose cleared her throat. 'Our great-great-grands had many shambas in Moshi, where the weather is cool and the night sky is a black wonder. They lived with views of the magnificent mountain day and night. Night and day.'

I stretched out onto my back, preparing myself for a long night of my own.

'Hmm,' Aunt Rose said after a second of silence. 'You know what a shamba is, yes?' I shrugged, which Aunt Rose read correctly as a no.

'*Eih, Baba,*' she scolded.

I hid my smug smile, happy that Baba was in trouble for a change.

'It's a farm,' she said.

OK. Baba had talked about the family farm but he'd never called it a shamba or said anything about a moun-tain so as far as I was concerned, I was still being honest. The room went silent again.

The window shook and I pulled my sheet up even higher. It was a cool night and I shivered into the sheets before turning to my side.

'Are you cold?' Aunt Rose asked.

I shrugged again. Aunt Rose read that correctly as a yes.

She got out of bed and fished something out of her suitcase, which was tucked in the corner of the room. She came over to my bed with a piece of fabric folded in her hands. She sat next to me and unfurled it. It was white with small blue dots and a purple flower motif twisting around all four sides. 'Read here.' She pointed at words printed in a small box just above the flower border at the bottom.

I had to sit all the way up to see the words properly, and then finally it happened.

I opened my mouth and talked.

'*A-mani. U-pendo. U-moji*?' I said, with hesitation in my voice.

I arched an eyebrow, waiting for a translation.

Aunt Rose grinned. 'This is called a kanga. We wear them wrapped around our bodies and tied at the neck. Or like shawls. Or head coverings. Many, many things. But they also have our sayings on them. Our proverbs. There are so many of them, in every colour combination, with very smartly written words. This is one of my favourites. I was saving it to give to you at the right time. *Amani* is peace. *Upendo* is love. *Umoja* is unity.'

I took the kanga and ran my fingers over the cotton.

It felt soft to the touch. 'Thank you,' I said, finding my manners.

Aunt Rose spread the kanga open wider. 'Use it to keep a bit warmer.' Then she slipped back into her bed and turned off the light. I could hear her shuffling her body down when another clap of thunder shook the room.

'Goodness,' she said. 'As if the sky was commanding me. Signs are everywhere, Kamaria.'

First rituals, then rhythm *and now* she was reading signs.

Maybe Aunt Rose and I did have some things in common.

She snuggled under her sheet. 'Now, back to the story about our great-great-grands who lived in Moshi in the shadows of the snow-capped Mount Kilimanjaro and who had many, many shambas . . .'

The thunder continued to make a big show, keeping me awake for at least another twenty minutes of Aunt Rose's story. As soon as the rumbles started to die down though, I could feel my breath slowing. The last thing I remember hearing about was a goat . . . and a tea plantation. . . and the old women . . . and the eastern slope of the mountain . . . before the sound of Aunt Rose's voice lulled me into a deep, deep, deep sleep.

24.
T MINUS
SEVEN DAYS

On Saturday morning I found Momma and Aunt Rose in the kitchen chitchatting away and drinking tea like sisters, which I guess they were. I plopped down and joined them, even though I still wasn't in the mood for talking.

I delivered my greetings and rested my chin in my palm. While they kept on catching up, I mulled everything over.

An electric bolt jolted me when I thought about Odie.

I hated being in the dark.

Would it ever end?

And so far, all I had to show for the chant was a sheet of paper with a few words scribbled on it. I still hadn't come through with anything solid.

The regional meet was in exactly seven days.

The state championship was soon after.

Doubt – *no, red-hot panic* – was starting to creep in.

After a minute, I turned to Aunt Rose, who perked up even more. She reached out for my hand and, turning back to Momma, laughed breezily at something without skipping a beat. Like she'd been with us from the get-go.

I was still warming up to Aunt Rose, but I'd let my guard down some.

Not that I had a choice.

Aunt Rose was moving full speed ahead. It helped that she was actually nice.

She wore her smile the way most people wore clothes. Every day, all day.

The sweet smells of vanilla and cinnamon radiated from her skin.

And the only thing she seemed to love more than cooking was talking.

Aunt Rose's hand lifted from mine and fell back into her lap.

There was a lull in the conversation. Suddenly all eyes were on me.

'How are all the girls?' Momma asked. She got up from the table and walked to the sink with her teacup and saucer. She ran the faucet and washed them. Momma couldn't stand dishes in the sink, which meant she hand-washed things all day long. Which meant we never used the dishwasher.

The one appliance worth its weight in gold.

'They're good,' I said, listening to the dishes clink and clank.

Aunt Rose smiled in her never-ending way. 'Mama tells me they're like your sisters, which is very nice since you don't have your own.'

I nodded and smiled.

Aunt Rose stood up, placing a hand on my shoulder before she walked over to the stove. I followed her with my eyes as she rolled up her sleeves. I hadn't noticed the pot simmering on the hob, but once she lifted the top and stirred, *whoa*, I could smell the coconut-tomato-ginger aroma rising.

My stomach turned in happy circles, it smelled so good.

'Mama says there are three, yes, Kamaria?' Aunt Rose stealthily pulled a handkerchief from her bosom and dabbed at a drop of sweat in her brow. She tucked the small cotton square away and kept stirring. I was still getting used to her saying Mama instead of Momma and Kamaria instead of Kam.

'Yup. Alexis, Luce and Neeka,' I answered.

Aunt Rose turned the sauce down low and spun around to face the big island we had in the middle of the kitchen. It was covered in flour. She pulled a kitchen cloth off of ten little balls of dough, smooth as a baby's bottom, which were resting on top of it.

I sat back and watched.

I guess the tea drinking and chitchatting were a pause in what looked like a full feast in production. Momma finished drying her hands on her pants. She shifted over a few feet from the sink and pressed the red button on the blender.

It whirred in the corner until Momma stopped it.

I wasn't sure what she was mixing, but the flavours smelled good too.

She turned around. 'Don't worry. I'm following Aunt Rose's careful instructions. Nothing will burn.'

I wasn't so sure.

Aunt Rose picked up the rolling pin and went to work – smashing each one of the little doughy balls down with her palm and then quickly rolling them out flat like pancakes. 'Mama says you have a big race coming. Is that so?'

'Yup,' I said. 'Next weekend.'

I don't know why, but I started telling Aunt Rose about the girls and our meets.

'I can't wait to see you fly down the runway,' Aunt Rose said, excitedly, using runway instead of straight-away. Then she broke out into song as loudly as she dared, like she was leading the eighth graders in a performance of *Les Misérables*. And she danced while she did it, too, swishing her dress to her knees.

Momma and I looked at each other and laughed.

Aunt Rose smiled showing all her teeth. 'Is there something that I can cook you to help you prepare? A favourite meal?'

'Oh,' I said, scratching an itch in between my braids. 'That's OK. I have a whole ritual the night before. I eat the same thing every time. Momma makes it.'

It was the one thing she made just how I liked it.

Momma started pulling down plates from the cabinet

and stacking them on the counter. She walked over in my direction and on her way to the pantry said, 'Aunt Rose is a much better cook than I am as you know. You could try it?'

I glared at Momma. 'You want me to try something new, the night before the regional championship?'

Momma turned around and threw her hands up in surrender. 'It was just a suggestion, Kam. Geez.' She turned to Aunt Rose. 'She's *very* superstitious.'

Aunt Rose winked at me. 'I completely understand.'

She moved to the front of the island and lifted a floury finger then spun back to the stove and turned on the two back burners.

Blue flames flared.

'Remember the kanga I gave you,' she continued. I nodded. 'One of the reasons why it is my favourite is because of the meaning of the words.'

'*Amani. Upendo. Umoja,*' I said out loud, trying to get them right. Peace. Love. Unity.

Aunt Rose nodded. 'Good job. You've even said them perfectly.'

I could only catch Momma's profile but I saw a smile tugging at her lips.

She loved that Aunt Rose was schooling me.

Aunt Rose continued. 'All of them. Good things. They represent what we need in our families, in our communities, and in our countries. Of course, in ourselves, too. A simple reminder.'

'I guess so,' I said.

'Sometimes that is enough to keep you focused,' Aunt Rose said a few seconds later, her back still to me. 'Just three little words.'

As Aunt Rose's hands flashed like quicksilver in their own rhythm and flow – in and out of pots, slicing and dicing, pulling and kneading – a small light started flashing in my mind.

It was trying to show me something.

But what?

Something about simple reminders to keep focused.

And me and the girls.

And running.

Which meant winning.

I couldn't pin point what it was exactly, but I was pretty sure it was for the chant.

I could feel it.

25.
ALL THINGS
ARE POSSIBLE

On Monday morning, I asked Momma to drop me off at school early.

Deserted early.

Before the sounds of teachers.

And morning bells.

And a mob of kids.

Early enough to hear the coo-cooing of the birds in the trees at the far end of the track and nothing else.

Being on the track was the best way for me to clear out the cobwebs from my head and find some rhythm. Especially since the flicker of light that had started flashing in my head after the conversation with Aunt Rose on Saturday.

I walked through the chain-link gate and made my way to my favourite spot.

The grass in the middle of the oval was freshly mowed and shiny with dew.

It smelled just like spring.

Which smelled just like track meets.

Which smelled just like winning.

I reminded myself of something Baba always said.

All things are possible.

Baba never explained what he meant by it, but I figured he meant having faith. Which I definitely needed to have right now.

I reached the starting line and bent over to stretch out my legs.

I crouched down on one knee and took a deep breath.

I raised my back leg . . .

My muscles tightened into knots and a touch of the nerves rattled my bones . . .

CLICK. CRACK. BOOM!

My feet struck the red track like lightning.

All the air flew out of my lungs like a rocket.

My heart thumped and pumped – shooting blood to every part of my body.

Ba-boom-ba-boom-ba-boom.

I crossed the finish line with my chest out and my arms up and my soul soaring.

My head was cool, crisp, clear.

My eyes were set on the target:

Write the chant.

Run the race.

Win first place.

Then, we'd be connected forever.

All things were possible . . .

26.
T MINUS FIVE DAYS

Second period ended early, so I used the gap to sit in Latin and ponder.

I had a good ten minutes before everyone rushed in.

I needed every one of them to try to stitch the threads I had together.

The first of our last two meets was in just five days.

My mind drifted from one idea to the next.

After a second, I opened my binder and quickly jotted something on a piece of loose-leaf paper. Just as I was mulling over the tip of another idea, Alexis slipped into the seat next to me and broke my train of thought.

Time was up.

I turned to face her.

She leaned over towards my desk, smoothing the stray hairs on the back of her head up into her ponytail. A smile fell over her face. 'What are you working on?'

I quickly covered my hands over the sheet of loose-leaf paper in front of me. 'Mind your business.'

'*Whaaaaat?*' Alexis said, squealing and bouncing in her seat. 'It's the chant. I know it. Here we go!'

I rolled my eyes for show, but was almost as excited as she was.

On the piece of paper that I didn't want Alexis to see, I'd scribbled:

Kam aka Wild Thing
Alexis aka Dum Dum
Luce aka Pip Pip
Neeka aka Poor Georgie

I had other ideas floating around, but our nicknames helped keep my focus.

We didn't get them all at the same time.

They kind of just happened one by one.

Usually because of something we did or said.

I was Wild Thing because of my crazy thick hair, which broke Neeka's comb when she was trying to wrestle it down into three cornrows one time before a meet. Alexis was Dum Dum because it didn't make any sense how smart she was, and we started calling Luce Pip Pip after we found out she'd been shouting pip pip hooray instead of hip hip hooray the whole time. Neeka used to be Purple Rain, after her favourite musician, but we swapped it out for Poor Georgie since she'd been playing that MC Lyte song like her life depended on it.

'I'm going to let the chant simmer with you for now,' Alexis said, smiling and scooting her chair closer to her desk. She pulled a purple notebook from her bag. Her name was written across the top of it in pretty curlicue letters. She looked back at me. 'But later, you have to throw me a bone. I'm dying over here.'

I smirked.

'Now, in other news,' she continued. 'What project did you decide to do for the Night of Learning?'

'Still not sure,' I said.

Everyone had to do a project for the Night of Learning, but we weren't actually graded on them. And there were no prizes.

The project was a way for us River Park students to share with our families something we'd learned.

Something that we thought was interesting.

In fifth grade, I made bottle rockets.

Last year, I made glow-in-the-dark slime.

This year's theme was *A Beautiful, Beautiful World*.

Each grade had a different sub-theme.

The eighth graders had the best one: *The Magic and Mystery of Outer Space*.

Ours was *Unique Landforms and Bodies of Water*.

We had to make a travel brochure convincing someone to visit a destination of our choosing, with a diorama of miniature life-like details.

Every year, I loved the Night of Learning, partly because Odie and I worked on our projects together.

Now, it just seemed like another thing we weren't doing together.

Another way I'd be kept on the outside of his world.

'Actually,' I added a minute later, looking at Alexis. 'I'll probably just do the Grand Canyon. You?'

Alexis stared back at me like my idea was as dry as a piece of dust. 'Something from Barbados, obviously. Mount Hillaby is pretty boring. I need something with more panache. Maybe the stalactites and stalagmites in Harrison's Cave. They have that wow factor.'

I was nodding at Alexis like a robot when Patrol walked into class carrying a handful of coloured folders. His combover was perfectly placed and he was wearing a plaid propeller bow tie around his neck. We called Mr Guilfoyle 'Patrol' because of the way he walked up and down the aisles and hallways, patrolling for trouble.

Patrol placed the folders on his desk and turned around to write on the board.

It would take him exactly two minutes to jot down the words of the day.

They were worth five points of extra credit.

Alexis quickly looked up at the board as the chalk squeaked, and then turned back to me. 'So yeah. The cave. But the Grand Canyon, Kam? Kinda whack.'

She gave me a thumbs down just as Patrol sat down at his desk. He glanced at his watch and then asked us to open our notebooks. He'd written three Latin words on the chalkboard: *esse*, *amare* and *posse*.

'Please write down the meaning of these three verbs,' he said. 'For those of you who want to go the extra mile and receive a whopping fifteen extra points, feel free to conjugate them.'

Someone booed.

'Without opening your dictionaries,' he added quickly, scanning the room.

'No kidding,' another person shouted.

The class quickly dissolved into near-chaos laughter. Patrol peered over his glasses and looked towards the back of the room where the racket was loudest. He straightened his already perfect bow tie and raised an eyebrow.

I whispered to Alexis, 'Do you think all the posses know about the Latin origins of their name?'

Turning to me, she whispered back, 'Haha.'

Patrol must have heard us because his gaze drifted in our direction. '*Girls*,' he said, with a warning look.

I looked back down at my binder with a serious face. I only knew what one word meant, so I wrote it down. I peeked at Alexis's notebook. It looked like she guessed all three, and conjugated them to boot.

After a few minutes, Patrol said, 'Pencils down. Who wants to give it a go?'

Alexis straightened up in her chair. Which meant she was about to show her smarts. Alexis almost always raised her hand first, and Patrol almost always waited to see if another hand would shoot up before he called on her.

He scanned the room.

His eyes settled on the front row. 'Alexis?' he said, giving in.

'*Posse* means "to be able". *Esse* means "to be". And *amare* means "to love".'

'You are correct,' he said, looking kind of mad about

it. He tapped his pencil on the desk. 'Am I correct in my assumption that you conjugated them as well?'

Alexis smiled yes with her eyes. While Patrol thumbed through the pages of our textbook, looking for where we left off yesterday, suddenly, all the tiny threads I'd been collecting started weaving themselves together.

Posse. Esse. Amare.

Three short words . . .

Easy to remember . . .

Just like Aunt Rose's favourite kanga.

Amani. Upendo. Umoja.

Peace. Love. Unity.

Upendo. Amare.

Love.

My brain was on fire now, finally in a good way.

The four of us loved running.

With our hearts and our souls.

But we also used our heads.

We plotted and we planned for our races. Well, I did.

We also kept track of our times. That was all Neeka.

We tried to keep cool heads, thanks to Alexis.

And Luce came up with the best zingers!

I looked at Alexis and whispered, 'The four of us use our brains, right?'

Alexis looked at me deeply annoyed. 'What are you talking about?'

Patrol looked over in our direction again.

But this time, instead of being worried about it, I wanted to shout out, 'Thank you, Patrol!'

I didn't.

I just kept pretending to pay attention and stayed in my groove.

Because I'd just figured it out.

Everything we put into running:

Our hearts. Our heads. Our souls.

I said the words in my mind, over and over again to see if they stuck.

Heart. Head. Soul. Heart. Head. Soul. Heart. Head. Soul.

Yup. That was it.

The beginnings of our chant.

The key to winning and cementing our bond forever.

27.
BEGINNING
TO END

After practice, I went straight to my room because the vibration was rumbling fast through my head and I wanted to write it out.

I sat down and rubbed my socked feet together under my desk.

I cracked my knuckles.

Then I pulled out my special notebook, the one for final drafts, and got started.

I had just written down the word 'we' when Aunt Rose flew into the room.

'Come, come, Kamaria,' she said, plonking down on her bed. 'I want to show you how I made the *biryani* rice.'

Aunt Rose liked to explain everything – from what she was cooking, to why they did certain things back in Tanzania. She even explained the reason for folding the corners of the sheets on the bed the way she did.

(It made a snugger fit and looked neater and was how her grandmother taught her). Turned out, it was nice to know more about how things were done in Tanzania, especially since Big Case Baba was still burning the midnight oil at work and barely had time to talk.

But I didn't need to know today.

And definitely not now.

I moved my wrist over my paper and swivelled my head in Aunt Rose's direction. 'Maybe next time, Aunt Rose. I have something important to finish up.'

Aunt Rose smiled. She pointed to my paper with her lips. 'Homework. I see.'

'Kind of,' I said.

'I enjoyed school. Although I didn't make it to university.'

I nodded and clenched the pencil tighter in my hand.

'The arts are my passion now, but in secondary school science was my best.'

I took a deep breath and smiled. 'That's great, Aunt Rose.'

'And can you guess what I loved learning about most?'

I shook my head while trying to keep the hum of the chant steady in my head.

It was hard, but so far, I was doing it.

Clap, clap, clap. Head, heart, soul.

Aunt Rose smiled hugely this time. 'The human heart.'

Lord, why did she have to look so happy to be talking to me?

I dropped my pencil and my shoulders.

The almost-solid-definitely-winning-super-chant bouncing around in my head would have to wait.

'When I was a kid,' I said, backing my chair out from my desk and turning to face Aunt Rose. 'I liked hearts, too. Apparently, I was always trying to find the sound of a heartbeat. Like in everything. Even things that weren't alive.'

Aunt Rose chuckled, easing herself back on the bed. 'Of course, you did. You like to travel deep into the heart. You like close connections. It is something we have in common.'

I smiled at Aunt Rose, always thinking she knew me.

'Anyway,' she continued. 'I don't remember much of what I learned. But I remember this. A very important thing. The human heart has four valves. They all connect, but each valve has its own role. Together, they control the way blood flows. But they all have to work together.'

I scrunched my face, all the while nodding.

The four heart valves were just like the four of us girls!

We each had a role to play on our 4 x 100 relay team.

Together, we would control the flow on the track.

The win would connect us forever.

My heart was racing.

No way was this a coincidence.

It was a sign.

A sign to say I was moving in the right direction.

To give me confidence and more gas.

And then just like that – *boom* – it was done.

I could finally hear the full-blown chant from beginning to end.

I'd found my groove.

My zing.

My rhythm.

Our rhythm.

I felt so relieved, I thought I might burst.

I closed my eyes and felt something else, too.

That sharp whip of air circling me and the girls as we flew around the track.

We were unstoppable.

28.
THE LONGEST
PAUSE ON EARTH

Much later that night I snuck downstairs and walked to the phone in the hallway. I was hoping Alexis would answer.

I was on a roll.

Luck was on my side.

'Can you talk?' I asked when I heard her scratchy voice.

'Oh yeah, I'm just eating dessert.'

'Dessert?' I sat down on the wooden floor and wrapped the long, coily phone cord around my feet. 'Didn't you eat dinner hours ago?'

'Yeah. This is my second dessert. First one was sweet but you know salty is my thing.' A pause. 'Hold on? How are you on the phone right now?' Alexis knew all of Baba's rules. Especially the one about no phone calls after 8 p.m.

'It's very important,' I said firmly, seizing on my new-found confidence.

Alexis snorted. 'What's not important with you?'

The phone went silent for a few seconds, then Alexis yelled, 'Get *ouuuuttaa* here.' I pulled the handset from my ear. 'Sorry,' she continued. 'My nephews. You know what freaks they are. PJ has underwear on his head.' Two years ago, Alexis's sister had twins and named them Patrick James and James Patrick: PJ and JP. When Alexis introduced them for the first time, she shook her head and said, 'I know. Don't say it. Dessa is so dumb.'

'On his *head*?' I asked, shaking my own. 'There is no good reason for them to still be awake. Don't kids need to be asleep by 5 p.m. or their brains won't grow or something? And are you in the closet again?' Alexis usually took her calls in the closet next to the kitchen because she didn't have privacy anywhere else.

'Yup,' she said. 'This place is my very own slice of heaven. Isn't that what Luce said about Zandy's Candy Store when we went that one time?' We both chuckled at the thought of Luce. 'And about the twins. Too late. They're already nuts.'

'So,' I said, playing coy. 'There's this big thing I have to do.'

'Oh, lord. Is this about having another chat with Odie? You two give me a migraine.'

I sucked my teeth. 'Not about O. About our chant.'

After Aunt Rose had finished telling me about the heart, and after she'd brought me downstairs to show me step-by-step how she made her fragrant rice, and after we'd eaten dinner as a family, and when Momma, Baba and Aunt Rose were watching TV and I FINALLY had some privacy of my own, I'd got to work, writing out all the words together, just like I'd heard them in my head. I tried to keep it simple, like Aunt Rose's favourite kanga, slowly peeling away words and sounds until it was just the essence of us and nothing more. I stood up from my papered desk an hour later with something that I thought felt true.

I deep inhaled. And then deep exhaled.

'Oh, OK,' Alexis said. 'Where you at? You got something good?'

I squeezed my toes in my slippers. A minute ago, I was sure the chant was something good. But now that I had to say it out loud to someone else . . . who knew?

'Kinda sorta,' I said, my confidence fizzling.

'Kinda sorta.' She let out a high-pitched squeal. 'OK, can I hear it? Hold on . . .' I heard Alexis cover the phone . . . then muffled voices . . . then Alexis whispered, '*Out.*' I imagined through clenched teeth. She came back on the line. '*All right, all right, all right!* I pushed a box of crap in front of the door. *Gogogogogogo!* I can only hold them off for so long. They *will* attempt a break in.'

'Well, I gotta set it up right. Situate you. Tell you the steps—'

'Kam, you can't plot everything. You gotta learn how to do things on the fly.'

I deep inhaled for the hundredth time. 'OK.'
And then I spat it out:

We got head deep – clap, clap, clap
We went heart deep – clap, clap, clap
We dug soul deep – clap, clap
To win this meet – clap, clap, clap

The phone sounded like it went dead. 'Alexis? . . .
Alexis?'

The longest pause on earth.

'ALEXIS?'

I heard a rustling sound and then a kid screaming
bloody murder.

Leave it to the rugrats to ruin a moment.

'Sorry about that. I swear I was listening and heard
the whole thing. You wanna talk about situate? I just
had to situate my feet like a barricade against the door!
KAAAAAAM!' Her voice screeched. 'I absolutely loved it.'

I stopped holding my breath. 'You think it's good?'

'No, I know it is. The way you like words and for how
long it took you, I thought it was going to be too fancy.
But nope. Head, heart, soul and all that good stuff. Four
lines, one for each of us. Simple but on point.' More
corn chips chomping in my ear. 'Maybe you could've said
something about our feet.'

I sighed, worried that I'd missed something.

'*But nah* . . .' Alexis said, settling the matter. 'It's
perfect. Nothing can stop us now. I can practically taste

121

the salty-sweet reward I'm gonna eat after we snatch that first place.'

I exhaled. 'Good.'

'So,' Alexis said, with a whole bunch of excitement in her voice. 'I think we just have to say it a few times. Build it up. Start out hushed and then get louder and louder. *School Daze* them. What do you think?'

I nodded my head even though Alexis couldn't see me and even though I hadn't been allowed to watch the movie *School Daze*. But I think I knew what she meant.

'I like that idea,' I said, in a happy daze myself.

'Hold on,' Alexis said. 'We have to call Luce first on three-way. And then Neeka.'

'Wait, can't I just tell it to them tomorrow at practice?'

'*What?*' Alexis said, her voice booming. 'Are you out of your mind? You're already on the phone. Already broke Kessy law. You wrote us a chant for the ages, Kam. They've gotta hear it tonight!'

29.
T MINUS ONE DAY

The rest of the week was a blip and before I knew it, it was Friday.

The last practice before the regional meet.

The four of us sat side by side with the rest of the team while Coach got into preacher mode.

'OK, girls,' he said, clapping his hands and buzzing around us like a bee. 'Listen up. We've made it. The regional championship is here. We've worked hard all season. We've had some losses. But we've had more wins. Most of all, you young ladies have shown grit and determination. Now is the time to pull it all together. Tomorrow is a big meet, but you have to treat it like any other race. Don't get wound up. That's when you make mistakes and get wobbly. Just focus on doing what you've done all season. Giving it your best. ARE YOU WITH ME?'

He shouted the last part.

We all nodded.

'We're gonna keep it tight and light today, but pick back up with our race-pace workouts next week so we can keep your wheels spinning. We don't want your legs or arms to get too relaxed because then it'll be hard to wake them back up come state championship time, which I know you're all itching to get to. But we'll cross that bridge when we get to it.' He looked around at all of us. 'And get a good night's rest for tomorrow. OK?'

Everyone nodded even harder.

Coach clapped twice. 'All right,' he said. 'We have a few more minutes before the track is cleared. Then we're good to go.'

'We don't need sleep,' Luce said, shooting up first. 'We have Kam's chant!'

'*Our* chant,' I said picking at the grass. 'It took me long enough. But I'm glad I got it done. I like it, too.'

'Like?' Luce said. She pulled me up and put her arm around me. 'It's dope. Simple and super fresh. We're gonna be flying to the finish line!'

The whole time Coach was preaching, all I could do was thank my lucky stars that I'd come up with something.

That the girls loved.

That felt like us.

That we'd practised for three days straight.

Still, it didn't keep at least a little fear from clawing up my chest.

Neeka bounced up, lifting her heels. 'OK,' she said, raising her eyebrow with a smirk. Then she got a serious look on her face. 'Let me give credit where credit is due. It is good. Especially considering how basic it is. Basic in a good way. Basic in the best way. Basic as in you better know your basics. As in we going back to the basics. As in we got our foundation straight. As in we're gonna be shaking all the way to first place.'

She shook her shoulders to match.

'Well,' I said, bending over and touching my toes to hide my stupid grin. 'I gave it my all.'

Alexis put her arm around me as soon as I straightened up. 'And your all is gonna send us home with that blue ribbon!' She pinched my left cheek.

'*Oww*,' I said, pulling away. 'Do I look like JP and PJ?'

'Kinda,' Alexis said. 'With that dusty look on your face.'

Luce and Neeka laughed.

A minute later, Coach blew his whistle, and we sprinted onto the track.

30.
CLOCKWORK

Every race night, I had my own ritual. And it ran like clockwork.

Momma made the one thing she never, ever burnt: my good luck dinner of banana flapjacks and biscuits.

Then, for dessert, I counted out ten red jellybeans from the glass jar in Baba's study. Baba retied the laces on my running shoes and put them downstairs by the front door, facing the street. On some mornings, I woke up to find the sun shining through the stained-glass window and it was like looking at my shoes with kaleidoscope vision.

That was extra good luck.

But the main thing was that I kept in my stride and did everything in order.

Tonight was the same, although Aunt Rose was confused about the eating part.

'So, it's *bread*?' she had asked at dinner. She scrunched up her face at my plate. It was the same race-night dinner I'd always had.

'It's not bread, Aunt Rose. It's flapjacks and biscuits.'

Aunt Rose sniffed. 'If this is what Mama and Baba have been feeding you all this time, who am I to say anything.' She shrugged her shoulders in defeat.

After dinner, I raced up to my room and left the grown-ups downstairs.

Aunt Rose, who couldn't take a hint, but definitely understood rhythms and rituals, winked at me just before I left. 'I will stay down here very, very late with Mama so I don't disturb you. No singing. No stories. Not a peep. I will enter the room quiet as a church mouse.'

Still, by the time I found myself in bed, I had a twinge in my stomach.

I snuggled myself deeper under the covers.

Half of me couldn't wait for the race. I wanted to know: would the chant really work?

Would it help keep us in sync and leave all the other teams in the dust?

Would we finally come first?

The other half of me was scared for morning to come.

What if the chant didn't work?

What if we lost?

What if we came in dead last?

My throat tightened.

During dinner, Aunt Rose had told me to try and relax.

Easy for her to say, though.

She was relaxed about everything.

The total opposite of me. And Big Case Baba, who was anything but relaxed at dinner. Momma had to pull him out of his office once all the food was on the table, but as soon as we were done, he kissed my head and flew straight back to his papers.

At least I knew he'd be there tomorrow cheering me on.

That's what I had to stay focused on.

Tomorrow.

I channelled my thoughts back to the track.

My chest rose as we shouted out the chant like a four-part harmony.

My stomach fluttered, just like it always did right before I bolted down the straightaway. The baton pass was picture-perfect and we didn't fumble.

Neeka flew across the finish line in first place.

We won!

I kept circling and circling around the track in my head until my eyelids felt extra heavy.

I was almost as good as gone, in the fuzzy space between awake and asleep, when a niggling thought lit up the dark.

Odie.

I hadn't spoken to him tonight.

He didn't usually call me before regular meets to wish me good luck.

But he always called before big ones.

Like tomorrow.

A chill swept across the back of my neck.

My mind wobbled.

Did that mean things hadn't gone like clockwork?

That was the last thing in my head before I drifted off to sleep.

31.
RACE FACES

'Race faces on!' Coach Rosse said as the bus lurched to a stop. We made it to the regional meet after a bumpy, hour-long drive. Coach got off first and gave each one of us a high-five before we sprang off the last step. A light breeze fluttered across my face and I wondered how hot it was going to get.

I was hoping we'd get a lucky break.

The last thing we needed was punishing heat.

I hitched my backpack up higher over my shoulder and watched busloads of other athletes walk into the stadium.

Different coloured uniforms whizzed on by.

Red-black-blue-purple-green.

I thought our team colours, black and orange, set us apart.

Even our nails were painted in them for team spirit.

The girls didn't share my zest.

Alexis and Luce agreed with Neeka who said, 'We look like Halloween running down the lanes.'

As we approached the top curve of the track, trying to play it cool, we passed by a bunch of twitchy-looking boys and girls – twisting and turning and jumping and stretching.

Some we recognized. Lots we didn't.

There had to be at least twenty different middle school teams.

We charged forward in our pack while a million bodies and loud noise swirled around us in all directions. It was like we were travelling through a huge static roar. The air was so thick with tension some coaches already had on their mean faces.

Lucky for us, Coach Rosse stayed calm and collected on race days.

With him, it felt like we were in the eye of a storm.

The safest part.

Eventually we made it all the way to the stands at the far end of the track.

The seats weren't crammed full like they would be at the state championship, but they still hummed loud enough to know that something big was about to happen.

Usually by the time the relays rolled around at the end of the meet, the crowd would be electrified.

We climbed the steps in silence and found our seats.

I took a deep breath as I dropped my bag.

It thumped

'You good?' Luce asked, unwrapping a Starburst.

I nodded while she popped the small red square in her

mouth and puckered her lips. Coach always warned us about eating candy before we ran.

Luce always ignored him.

'Want one?' she asked, holding out the pack.

I shook my head, no.

She went back to chewing, and laughing, and goofing and twirling her red curls.

Luce wasn't playing it cool, she *was* cool.

She always was at track meets.

I was in my head agonizing about every little thing.

A long day stretched ahead of us.

Not only did we have to run in the relay together, we each had our own individual events.

Itty-bitty Luce was a long jumper.

Alexis ran the hundred-metre hurdles.

Neeka and I ran the hundred-metre dash.

According to the official order of events, we'd have to get through *all* of our races first. Then we'd run in the relay, which was the second-to-last event of the meet.

Hours away.

'When are we gonna practise our chant again?' Luce asked as she rifled through her backpack. 'After the group warm-up?' We all knew repetition was how you made things stick.

'I guess so,' I said, my stomach flipping.

It was time to shift gears.

32.
SEA OF NERVES

After we finished a few laps around the grass, we ran back behind the stands. It was pretty empty compared to where all the action was.

Probably the calmest area in the whole stadium.

A small group of timekeepers stood around in windbreakers.

Some kids ran back and forth to the bathroom.

Announcements chirped in the background.

As we stood around in a huddle, I talked the girls through the meaning behind the chant and how Aunt Rose had helped me with it without even knowing.

Not even Alexis knew any of this.

Head deep was for our laser focus.

Heart deep was for our love of running.

Soul deep was for that invisible thing that kept our legs moving and us connected.

The last line was obvious. We came to win.

We started.

The four of us stood there together, sing-shouting and clapping.

Neeka to my left. Alexis to my right. And Luce straight in front of me.

Each of us took a line:

Neeka started. *We got head deep*. We all clapped three times.

Then Alexis. *We went heart deep*. We all clapped three times.

Next was Luce. *We dug soul deep*. We clapped twice.

I was last. *To win this meet*. Three more claps.

A few volunteers walked by, but nobody paid us any mind as we started out in a hush just like Alexis had suggested and then shouted out the chant with a beam of confidence that could reach the moon.

It was like we found our own secret calm place in a sea of nerves.

And a faster, fresher rhythm.

'I think we got it,' Neeka said, clapping quicker to match my rhythm and taking her voice down an octave.

Luce and Alexis picked up the pace and lowered their voices, too.

We got in a few more rounds, making sure each clap was as steady as a pulse, before the squawk of the PA system shook us out of our trance.

It was the first call for the long jump.

Luce's event.

She had to go warm up.

We all walked back together, except for Luce, who

was skipping. Her brick-coloured Shirley Temple curls skipping with her.

'I guess you're not nervous,' I said to Luce when we were back at the bleachers.

'Nope,' she said as she snatched up her backpack like someone on the run. 'You know I can jump in my sleep.'

Luce had come first almost every single meet that season. Being short was like her secret weapon. The other girls didn't expect someone so tiny to jump so far.

We each gave Luce a quick hug, and she ran off to the sandpit.

One by one, races were called.

I settled in for the long haul and pulled a book from my backpack.

Neeka pressed play on her Walkman and drowned out everything else.

Alexis sat around on high alert.

She knew she'd be called next.

Almost an hour later, Shari Wightman, another hurdler on our team, grabbed Alexis by the arm. 'We need to warm up now,' she said, carefully tip-toeing over our feet as she pulled Alexis with her.

I stood up and pulled Alexis in for a quick squeeze. 'Good luck,' I said, crossing my fingers.

Neeka stood up and gave Alexis a hug too. When she sat back down, she put her headphones over her ears and went right back to her head bop.

After *another* half hour of waiting, I heard the final call for Alexis's race.

It was happening now. I elbowed Neeka.

We both stuffed our things in our backpacks and zipped them up.

Everything would go quick now.

We stood up on our tippy toes and watched from the stands as Alexis took her spot at the starting line in lane four. When she crouched down, I lost sight of her behind the hurdles. Within seconds, though, she'd be popping up like a firecracker.

'Runners! Take your marks!' the official shouted.

The shot rang out. Alexis exploded from the line and attacked the first hurdle.

The white ribbons in her braids waved like flags.

Neeka and I jumped up and shouted, 'Go, Dum Dum!'

A few people looked at us sideways. We woo-hoo'd even louder.

Alexis's right leg shot up again and made it over the next hurdle.

And the next one.

And the next one.

She was almost half-way done. Eating up more space. In her rhythm.

By the fifth hurdle, Alexis was in second place behind Shari.

She'd have to shred the last five if she wanted to win.

When she cleared the last one, it was neck and neck. My heart pounded so fast it might as well have been me running.

Alexis dipped her head forward and flew across the finish line.

Neeka jumped.

The results were quickly announced.

Alexis came in second place. Just behind Shari.

Alexis and Shari hugged each other, then walked off the track, breathing hard.

Alexis's chest was still puffing by the time she climbed up to the bench and sat down next to us. She leaned forward and put her head between her knees.

'Pip Pip,' I started.

'*Hooraayy*,' Neeka finished.

Alexis sat up. 'You guys are so stupid.' We looked at each other and cracked up.

Alexis pulled a water bottle from her bag and guzzled.

The pressure was off her for now. She only had the relay left.

Neeka and I were just getting started.

We had to go run the hundred-metre dash now.

I gave Alexis one more hug before Neeka grabbed my hand and started pulling me down the aisle.

'Guys,' Alexis called after us, still gasping for air. We both turned our heads to look at her. 'Blow it out!'

33.
NIGHT AND DAY

'Do you remember them from the Northridge meet?' Neeka asked as we headed to our race. She pointed to a group of girls wearing navy blue singlets. All three of them had two French braids in their hair tied with ribbons in their school colours.

'Sort of,' I said, pinning my number to my chest. 'I think the one with dark hair is named Caroline or something.'

The girls jogged in front of us and waved. I waved back as I watched their long braids swish back and forth.

'Wait,' I said, remembering. 'Not Caroline. Her name is Brookline.'

'Oh yeah,' Neeka said. 'Anyway, Brookline is in your heat. She's definitely coming in the strongest. She's the one you have to beat.'

In some ways, Neeka and I were like night and day when it came to running.

On race days, she was like a scientist and a detective, all rolled into one.

She wanted cold, hard facts. She watched race times and heats.

She investigated who won and who lost.

Even as her feet hit the track, she was in her head.

For me, running a race was like being thrown far out into the galaxy.

A billion light years away.

Once my feet started moving, I could finally leave all the planning and plotting behind. I disappeared and became a heartbeat. Part of the earth and the sky and outer space all at the same time.

We walked closer to the waiting area.

'Anything else I need to know?' I asked.

'Nah. You got the rest.'

We high-fived and Neeka went to the starting line.

There were four heats for our race.

Neeka was in the first.

I was in the second.

There were two ways to make it to the final. We each had to win our heat.

Or, we had to have one of the top four fastest times out of all four heats.

Neeka's race was over before it started.

The other girls in her heat tried to chase her down, but they were no match.

She won it easy.

By some miracle, I beat Brookline and won my heat too.

Now, it was time for the hundred-metre final.

I tried to stay steady, even though I could feel my muscles clenching and my stomach roiling.

Breathebreathebreathe, I reminded myself.

'Good luck,' Neeka said. She hugged me and rolled her shoulders back.

She was completely unfazed.

Set to win.

I was hoping I'd be right behind her, but the competition was stiff.

I looked towards the bleachers. There were too many people for me to see Momma, Baba and Aunt Rose, who had been giddy with excitement this morning.

I gulped and got into position.

Twelve seconds later, the race was done and we were waved off the track.

34.
FLY GIRLS

Neeka slung her arm around my shoulder, grinning. 'Good race.'

'You too,' I said, between breaths of air. My pulse was still pounding all over my body and my mouth was as dry as cardboard.

I'd finished right after Neeka in second place.

I'd set a personal record, too.

My fastest hundred-metre time yet.

We walked toward the bleachers and up the stairs, still searching for oxygen in our lungs. 'You see your parents?' Neeka asked, scanning the stands.

'Not yet. You?'

We climbed past the fourth row and Neeka swung her head left. She made a hand sign to someone and grinned. 'That was just her. Well, not Ma. Dama.'

I stretched myself over Neeka's back and waved at her sister.

Dama smiled. There she was in a purple and gold

silk kimono top, bucket hat, and bamboo earrings. Just oozing her Lisa Bonet-coolness.

'I saw Dama's big head jumping up and down right when I finished too,' Neeka said. 'You know how she does that thing every meet where she sits four rows up, dead centre, so I always know where to fix my eyes when I'm done.'

I nodded, remembering all of their secret signals and codes.

I hoped our secret was getting ready to work its magic too.

When we found the team again, everyone cheered.

Our teammates shoved us back and forth as we made our way down the plank to our bags. Every point counted for the team prize and we'd taken the top two spots.

A lot of the other girls had done well too.

Our school team might actually take the regional championship title.

We finally got to Luce and Alexis, who were waiting for us.

'*Flyyyy giiiiiirls*,' Luce sang, drawing out the words.

She swatted Neeka with her sweatshirt and then gave me a hug.

'First place?' I asked, wrapping my arms around her tiny body. I lifted her up. If we weren't hemmed in by the bleachers, I would have carried her on my back like I usually did.

'You know it,' she said, her arms flailing around. 'I'm just standing in the winning spot, sucking on a lollipop.'

Her tongue was bright red from her Blow Pop.

And only Luce could spin a lyric from her favourite song around so fast like that.

'Spin it Spinderella,' Alexis joked.

'You mean LL,' Neeka jabbed, playfully.

'What about you Poor Georgie,' Luce shot back to Neeka.

I knew we were on fire once we started speaking our own language.

Last year, after riding home with us from a track meet, Odie told me it was probably time to call up Merriam-Webster. When I asked him why he said, 'Because the rest of us need a dictionary to understand you.'

Luce finished off by squeezing a dance in the tight space.

When her huge windbreaker hood fell down over her head, she looked just like a baby standing there with nothing but a lollipop sticking out of her mouth and a few of her red curls peeking through.

We were all in the moment, being silly and laughing.

But we still had one more race to win.

The relay.

35.
CHANT TIME

'So, you know not to look her in the eyes, right?' Neeka
barked, already in chop-chop mode. That's what we called
it when she was ready to cut someone down to size.

'Yes, we know,' the three of us answered.

We were walking towards the grass in the middle of
the track.

They'd already made the last call for the 4 x 100 relay.

Our race was about to start.

You'd think Neeka would have eased up by now.

She'd finished first in the hundred metres, after all.

But she was still edgy. I was the one flooded with relief.

We'd smashed our individual events.

We just had to maintain what we'd started.

That's why I wasn't sipping in air.

I was drinking it in. Taking whole breaths.

The little bombs in my stomach had stopped detonat-
ing and I wasn't thinking about Crazy-Cold Eyes, the girl
Neeka was obsessing about.

Her real name was Stasha Mitchell.

But we called her Crazy-Cold Eyes because she made the wildest faces when she ran. And because her cold eyes sliced through people like they were swords made of ice.

And because she could act stone-cold crazy.

She also happened to be the fastest seventh grader in our district.

She usually ran the individual one-hundred-metre dash with me and Neeka. But today she ran the four-hundred-metre, a full lap around the track.

And, of course, because she was Stasha Mitchell, she smashed it.

If Neeka had a rival – someone she just *had* to beat – it was Stasha Mitchell.

'OK!' Neeka said, after our quick pep talk with Coach Rosse. She dug her heels into the grass. 'Chant. Blast off. Win. In that order. Let's go!'

Then she clapped her hands twice, like Coach.

Energy bounced around us like pinballs.

The *boingboingboing* was springing in my head too!

I looked back at the crowd again to see if I could spy Momma, Baba or Aunt Rose, but there were way too many people now. I turned around and we pulled ourselves together in a tight circle, our heads touching.

Alexis and Luce were on either side of me.

I raised my head and met Neeka's chameleon-like eyes.

They were almost every colour in the rainbow.

It was chant time.

36.
RHYTHM IS KING

We decided to start together, each of us taking our lines in a hush. Then we would continue on our own, shouting and clapping our way to the starting line of our individual legs, our voices growing louder and louder with each round.

We got head deep – *clap, clap, clap*
We went heart deep – *clap, clap, clap*
We dug soul deep – *clap, clap*
To win this meet – *clap, clap, clap*

We finished the first round of the chant and fanned out across the track in perfect rhythm. I made it to the top of the straightaway, across from the starting line, and stood in position.

This was the one race where I knew Coach Rosse's eyes would follow the track like a hawk. He was already standing by the starting line, hat perched atop his head.

His stopwatch dangled loose from his neck.

I didn't meet his eyes.

Didn't look around. I just bounced up and down on my toes and waited.

The sound of the gun cut through the noise.

CLICK. CRACK. BOOM!

Everything fell silent.

There was no time to think.

Or hear.

Later on, I would say that was a good thing.

Because if my ears or my head had been working right, then I would've remembered every single second of every single thing going wrong right before my eyes. Here's what I *did* remember, at least, at first:

Alexis in first leg.

She was coming around the curve.

Knees flying.

Metal baton whipping up and down.

She was off to a great start.

No.

She was perfect.

The tunnel focus in her eyes.

The steady rhythm of her heel-toe, heel-toe, heel-toe, slapping against the ground.

I was ready. More ready than I'd ever been for anything.

As soon as Alexis hit the mark, I whipped my head around and took off.

My hand was back. *I swear it was.*

My palm was flat. My thumb was down. *I know they were.*

But where was the baton?

I flinched for a sliver of a second. Then finally I felt it cool in my palm.

Thank God.

But it was too late. As soon as it was in my palm, it slid right out.

I don't know if Alexis held the baton out too late or if I took off too early.

Either way, we were out of rhythm.

And rhythm is king.

Rhythm is EVERYTHING.

Or maybe I choked. Maybe I just choked.

The sound of metal bouncing against the track was the last thing I remembered before my whole universe went dark, then crumbled to dust.

Our fate was sealed.

37.
A BUNCH OF
BROKEN CHORDS

On Sunday afternoon, Momma came into my room and shook me awake. I kept the pillow over my head while letters strung together into words that might as well have been Klingon streamed out of her mouth. It sounded like she said I'd been sleeping for seventeen hours straight and I needed to get up. She knew I was devastated and that nothing she could say was going to make it any better. She and the rest of the family would be waiting for me downstairs.

The race was over, she said. But there was still today.

A wave of horror swept through me.

Who cared about today?

The last thing I wanted to face was today.

I walked into the kitchen like a robot, mumbled hello, grabbed a piece of French toast, ate it without chewing, and then put my head down on the table.

Aunt Rose started swirling circles on my back. '*Kipenzi*, are you OK?'

'No,' I grumbled.

'What can I do?' She stood up and wrapped herself around me from behind in a full body hug. If I wasn't on the verge of a meltdown, I would have laughed out loud.

'Nothing,' I mumbled instead.

Eventually Momma, Baba and Aunt Rose moved from the kitchen into the living room, while I lugged myself back upstairs.

I noticed the flowers by my bedside.

Momma must've put them there yesterday.

She thought flowers could fix anything.

Nope. Not this.

There was a cold cup of chai next to them with a cinnamon stick peeking out of the top. That was definitely Aunt Rose.

Tea wouldn't work either.

From my bedroom, in between the sound of the adults cackling, I could hear the phone ringing nonstop. I figured it was Alexis trying to get me to move past it already.

Or Luce trying to make fun of it and brighten my mood.

I knew Neeka wasn't trying to call.

Just saying her name made my head hurt.

I decided the best thing to do was to sleep it off, so that's what I did.

By the time I woke up for the second time, streetlights were on and my room was dark and lonely. I looked out of the window at a hidden half-moon. Being distracted seemed like a good idea, so I went back downstairs and followed the sounds coming from the living room. My instincts told me it was laughter, but to my ears it sounded like a bunch of broken chords.

Momma, Baba and Aunt Rose were sitting on the oversized couch watching TV.

They stopped laughing and got very straight-faced when they saw me.

Straightened up their backs too.

Baba picked up the remote and pressed mute.

A show with cheery people flickered in the background.

I glanced at the TV, pressing my toes into the soft carpet.

Momma came over and wrapped me in a hug. I leaned into her arms and took in her flowery scent. She pulled me to the couch and I scooched in between her and Baba.

Aunt Rose bent forward, reaching her arm around Momma.

She patted me on the leg.

I took in a deep breath and that's when it finally hit me.

We lost the second most important race of the season.

I lost the second most important race of the season.

I didn't want to talk about it, but I did want to know one thing.

I turned my head to Momma. 'Do you think everyone hates me?'

Momma and Baba exchanged worried glances. 'Of

course not,' Momma said a second later. 'Is that what you're worried about?'

Well, yeah. That and losing.

I shrugged, trying hard to blink back tears before they snuck out of my eyes.

It was hard to think about letting the whole entire team down.

The girls, especially.

Momma squeezed my shoulder. 'The phone has been ringing off the hook since we got home from the meet yesterday evening.' She let me go and bent over, scratching an itch on her bare foot. 'Alexis and Luce must have called twenty times each.'

'And Odie left a message,' she added, giving me a big smile.

Space cleared in my head for a minute.

Odie?

It couldn't get any worse.

I shoved the thought from my mind and held perfectly still, trying to blink back the tears.

And in the silence, I realized something.

She didn't say Neeka.

But I guess I already knew I could count on that.

Her *not* calling, that is.

'I'll call them tomorrow,' I told Momma, deep sighing. 'I just want to watch TV.'

Baba quickly pressed unmute and the folks on the screen laughed while we watched. Eventually, Momma, Baba and Aunt Rose were laughing again too.

152

By the end of the show, I almost laughed with them. But my heart wasn't in it.

38.
THE HARDEST THING
TO SWALLOW

Momma never let me stay home from school unless it was for something legit.

Which meant fever-sick. Not teary-bleary-eyed-sick.

But on Monday she bent her own rules.

Mainly so that I could let things settle down in my head, she said.

Even though it was my heart that had crumbled.

By the time I dragged myself out of my room and made my way downstairs, I was the only one there. Momma was down the hall in her office with a client, making someone else feel better or whatever it was psychologists did.

Baba was at work, protecting people's rights.

And Aunt Rose was back upstairs resting.

She'd spent the early morning hours baking up a storm.

When she slipped back into bed at 6 a.m. and found my eyes wide open, staring at the Olympic rings on my ceiling, she said, 'You'll be back to normal soon, *kipenzi*. I've prepared a little sweetness to take the stinging away.'

Little was an understatement.

When I walked into the kitchen it was like being transported to Rosie's Bakery downtown. Sprawled out on the island were two lemon cakes, a mountain of *mandazi*s, a batch of chocolate chip cookies and two trays of cinnamon rolls, with icing, made from scratch, to boot.

Momma had tried too.

She'd left a bowl of her crusty porridge for me on the counter.

I scooted right past it and grabbed a plateful of Aunt Rose's mandazi. They were still warm to the touch and smelled spicy, sweet.

I sat down at the kitchen table and tried not to think about Saturday as I tore into a doughnut and chewed and swallowed.

I was even tricked into a minute of pleasure as I ate.

Aunt Rose's mandazi were *definitely* better than any-thing Momma cooked.

Easier to swallow than the truth, too, which had hit me like a ton of bricks yesterday. Only now was it really sinking in, though.

The full weight of it pressing down hard on me.

I dropped the baton.

Not winning and coming in last place was bad enough.

155

But not winning and coming in last place because of *me*?

My breath quickened.

The whole thing all came flashing back from start to finish.

39.
EVEN BADDER

It all started with the four of us warming up, stretching and checking-in.

Then, Coach Rosse walking over to us and telling us he already knew we could get the baton around the track with a great time, but it was our hard work that he was proud of. Watching him stroll back to the starting line to wait offside with the rest of the coaches, his hat balanced on his head like a bird on a branch like always.

Then, the moment we'd been waiting for.

We had our chant. Our rhythm and flow.

The winning recipe.

It had to work.

Us shouting out with blinding excitement. Our heart-beats in sync for a few shimmering moments as the words echoed out across the track . . .

We got head deep – *clap, clap, clap*
We went heart deep – *clap, clap, clap*
We dug soul deep – *clap, clap*

To win this meet – clap, clap, clap

Us checking our marks and getting some running starts in.

My eyes gazing towards the stands.

Then bang.

The gun going off.

Alexis coming up on me, closer, closer, closer.

Her hitting the mark on the track that meant I should take off.

Me taking off.

And now I saw what I hadn't been able to see for two days.

Me afraid that Alexis was coming so quick she would run over me and I wouldn't get the baton in the exchange zone. And if I didn't, we'd be disqualified.

Me slowing down. Just a bit.

Me having a split second of doubt.

Me reaching back even more for the baton and not feeling it.

Me panicking . . .

Me finally feeling the baton just before it escaped my grip.

Me totally out of rhythm.

The cool baton slipping out of my hand like a slippery fish and crashing down onto the track. In a flash, five other teams whizzing by . . .

The first-place blue ribbon slipping through *all* our fingers.

But it didn't stop there . . .

Me remembering what Coach always said: Never give up.

Me picking up the baton and chasing down last place.

Luce in my front view yelling, 'Come on, Kam. You can do it. Faster!'

Me slapping the baton down hard in her hand and then bending over to catch my breath.

Luce taking off like a little rocket and handing off to Neeka.

Neeka running for her life.

And my life.

And all of our lives.

Neeka running as fast as the speed of light.

So fast you could barely see her on the track – you could only see a flash of her.

The race finishing with us, River Park, coming in dead last.

It was remembering the last part that made me stop chewing and swallowing.

My throat closed around a big lump of humiliation.

It was so big nothing was getting past it.

Not even Aunt Rose's mandazi.

Especially with what happened next.

We all met with Coach Rosse at the finish line.

He was the kind of coach that wanted to set things straight right then and there.

He always said we could walk away disappointed, but he wanted to see race faces on and chins up. Good sportsmanship was more important than winning.

According to him.

That's why even though we lost, we still had to con-gratulate the other teams with a parade of high-fives. My hands felt as heavy as lead as they smacked, smacked, smacked. My feet felt like lead too.

But I did like I was told and slapped on my race face.

Finally, we sat down on the grass in a half circle.

Alexis didn't say a word to me. Instead, she put her arm around my shoulder.

Luce put her arm around the other.

Sitting there between the two of them, I felt held together.

Propped up.

The way beams hold up a house.

Luce turned to look at me, her face so close to mine that I could smell her sweet, candied breath. 'At least we already qualified for the state championship,' she said. 'Don't worry! We still got one more shot.'

I couldn't think that far ahead.

And I didn't dare look Neeka's way.

She was still a streak of orange and black running down the track in my mind.

Coach squatted down. He rested his elbows on his knees and knitted his hands together. 'I know you're disappointed, and we'll have a chance to tease out what happened later, but I just wanted you to know this hap-pens. It wasn't the first time and it certainly won't be the last time you drop the baton on the track.'

He looked around at us. I could tell he was trying to read our faces.

I was only listening to Coach with half an ear.

But I heard Neeka loud and clear when she said, 'I didn't drop the baton, *Kam did*.'

Next came me hoping and wishing I would dissolve into a million atoms and vaporize into the air.

'That's enough,' Coach replied to Neeka sternly. He sat back on his heels. 'It's never about one person. And I know you know this. Why don't you all cool down properly and I'll see you back with the rest of the group. I know you're tired and more than ready to go home. But we have the last event, and you need to put your disappointment aside and support your teammates the way they've supported you.'

Neeka glowered straight into Coach's face, her eyes two tiny tempests.

I had the guts to look at her now, but still couldn't see her.

I could only feel the storm of her picking up strength.

I knew she would be raging soon.

Coach turned to me. 'Kam, your parents, aunt and Odie are sitting with us now. I'm sure you'll feel better once you're with them. But the meet isn't over. Keep positive. And don't forget to support your teammates.'

I took a deep gulp of air into my still-burning lungs.

Odie had come?

My whole body was on fire now.

When I found Momma and Baba in the stands, they

knew me well enough to leave well alone. Even Aunt Rose didn't say a word as I squirmed my way into the space between her and Odie. I looked straight ahead at the track and tried to think of what a disaster it must have looked like from up here.

'Hand,' Odie said, quick and quiet.

A shiver ran down my spine.

He elbowed me.

I slowly opened my palm without looking over.

Odie took his hand and laced his warm fingers through mine.

Instead of my heartbeat racing even more, it slowed.

And for half a second, I felt like myself.

Not rhythmless Kam. Not losing Kam.

Just Kam.

I'd summoned up the whole day so freshly in my mind I'd almost forgotten that I was still sitting in the kitchen in my PJs.

I stood up from the table, grabbed my plate, and dropped it in the sink.

I had a whole day in front of me.

A whole day to *try* to forget everything I'd just remembered.

Except for the hand.

There was no way I could forget that.

When Alexis and Luce called after school on three-way, Momma bent the rules again and let me speak on the phone until dinnertime. Thanks to Luce's genius-level playback skills, I had to sit through the entire mess all over again.

Blow-by-blow.

It was one thing to remember it myself, another thing altogether to hear someone else tell it.

Luce shared more details than I cared to know. Like when she said:

. . . and did you know that Crazy-Cold Eyes and them were standing so hard in their buffalo stance I could hear Neneh Cherry singing. They were all smirking and gleeful.

. . . Neeka said they even had the nerve to call us losers.

. . . Esabella said it wasn't your fault, but she DID say it was way worse than last year!

. . . I ran so fast my shoe almost fell off.

. . . Thank GOD I didn't fall. That would've made a bad situation even badder.

While Luce droned on, something sprang into my head.

How could I have believed in a chant?

It was stupid.

Silly.

Isn't that what Neeka first thought when I came up with the idea.

I guess she was right after all.

40.
SOMETHING RIGHT

Later, we ate dinner as a family in the formal dining room where sparkly crystals dripped down from the chandelier above the table.

Momma and Baba usually saved this room for entertaining.

Or my birthday parties.

Aunt Rose was still getting the royal treatment.

The dinner she made was so good I went for thirds.

I swallowed so quickly I could still feel the burn in my throat when I was done.

While Momma, Aunt Rose and Baba continued conversing, I forked the last bite of food into my mouth and ran down the list of all the things I couldn't compute.

Odie.

Why did he reach for my hand? *We'd never held hands before. Did that mean we were friends again?*

My mind rattled on to the next thing.

Neeka.

Would she ever forgive me?

I knew the answer to that one. Never and that was a fact.

The chant.

The biggest bust. If that didn't work, nothing would.

My rhythm

It was gone. And I'd probably never get it back.

With all that wrongness, it was getting hard not to think that something wasn't wrong with me. I put my fork down onto my plate, the taste of Aunt Rose's spicy chicken tingling my tongue.

Aunt Rose.

At least she was something right in my life.

When exactly did that happen? And how?

Baba stood. 'I haven't seen you so eager to help yourself in a long time, Kamaria.' He kissed me on the head as he carried our plates to the kitchen.

I shrugged.

I wasn't a kid any more.

A kiss from Baba wasn't going to solve my problems.

41.
LOUD MOUTHS
AND LOSERS

While the three adults watched TV, I went back to my room to stare blankly at the walls. I stayed stuck like that until I heard Momma calling me from the foot of the stairs. The phone had rung.

Momma had answered.

She had bent her rules *again*, letting me take the call even though I'd already spoken to Alexis and Luce for three hours before dinner.

She even let me talk in her office so I'd have complete privacy.

Before she closed the door and walked out, she looked at me and mouthed, 'It will be OK.' She gave me a thumbs up before disappearing behind the door.

I picked up the receiver and waited a few seconds for Momma to hang up the other one. 'Hello?' I said, once I heard the click.

'Why did it take you forever and a day?' Alexis asked. The rugrats were screaming in the background, as usual.

'It didn't.' I leaned back in Momma's desk chair, swivelling from left to right. And before Alexis could start, I cut to the chase, figuring she had more to add on to what Luce said. 'I know you and Luce are trying to help, but I really don't need to hear any more—'

'That's not why I'm calling,' she said, breathing heavy. 'Neeka's on the line too . . . Neek?'

I could hear Neeka huffing through the phone. 'Not my idea, Alexis. You better go 'head.'

After a long pause, Alexis said, 'Kam . . . Neeka . . . you two have to straighten this out. I know you haven't seen each other yet, but I'm hoping we can fix this before you do. Neeka, you know Kam didn't mean to drop the baton. Heck, it could've been my fault for all we know. Kam, what happened . . . *happened*. Let it go. And then we all need to get back to normal and focus on the real championship. The state meet. There.'

Neeka and I both groaned at the same time, our voices colliding over the line.

'Go 'head,' I said, letting Neeka go first. I rolled my chair forward and passed my fingers over the few things on Momma's absurdly tidy desk.

An ivory letter opener.

An amethyst paper weight.

A perfect stack of bills.

The most disorderly thing in her office was a small knot of paper clips sitting by a pencil holder.

'Maybe you didn't mean to drop the baton,' Neeka started. 'But you *did* drop it. *You* were the one who set it all up like winning was easy. *All we need is something extra. A chant. Listen to Coach. Do everything I say, and we'll win. Blah, blah, blah . . .*' I pictured her neck swirling in my mind. 'Well, we did everything you, the grand wizard, said instead of putting more time into our hand-offs and fast feet. Then *you* went ahead and messed—' I stopped spinning in Momma's chair, her words bringing me to a complete standstill.

'Talk about messing things up,' I cut in. 'You wouldn't still be on the team if I, the grand wizard, didn't always keep *you* straight. Maybe I dropped the baton because I was tired. Tired of always having to keep *you* from getting kicked off the team—'

Alexis jumped in. 'Wait guys. Can someone say sorry?'

'NO!' we both shouted. I guess we saw eye to eye on something.

'Loud mouth,' I grumbled under my breath.

'Loser,' Neeka said in a low hiss.

I froze. The only sound left was Alexis's groaning.

It took a second for me to feel the crush of the blow.

Isn't that what Luce said Crazy-Cold Eyes had called us?

My face grew warm, and my heart twisted in my chest.

I hung up.

A second later the phone bleated out again.

I took a steadying breath and picked it up before the ring finished.

'She didn't mean it,' Alexis said quickly.

168

Air huffed out of her chest like her heart was beating a hundred miles a minute.

I swallowed the sting in my throat. My eyes were burning. Hot tears started rolling down my cheeks. 'Yes, she did. I'll see you tomorrow.'

Alexis sighed, like she was carrying the weight of the world. 'All right.'

Neeka and I had our moods with each other, but we'd never said words that needed taking back. We were like sisters. And the number one unwritten rule of sisterhood? No throwing daggers.

I knew I threw the first one.

But when Neeka threw one right back, it cut deep.

Then it hit me in the face.

Neeka and I were teeter-tottering right on the edge of losing our friendship.

Just like I'd lost Odie.

Just like we were losing Luce.

Maybe losing was just my thing.

42.
CALL IT DESTINY

I sat at Momma's desk stunned at what had just happened and wondering how things had turned topsy turvy so fast. One minute Neeka and I were acting silly, doing the do-si-do at track practice. The next we were spitting fire at each other. It felt even worse because I could trace all of it – the girls, running, our flow – back to the day I met Neeka . . .

It was the first day of fifth grade.

Momma had me gussied up in her idea of Sunday best.

Which was any sane person's idea of Sunday worst.

I begged her to at least let me wear high-tops, but she wouldn't hear of it.

She stared at me so long and so hard in her quiet storm way that I dropped it.

I tucked my moaning and groaning away and took it with me.

All the way to the sidewalk where the school's emerald

green quad peeked out from behind a bricked archway. Momma gave me a kiss and pushed me along.

Odie would've been right by my side so we could walk in together like we'd done every year but he had the chicken pox and missed the first few days of school.

Call it destiny.

Neeka was marching into the quad at the exact same time I was. Except she was dressed head-to-toe in everything I wasn't: an all-white windbreaker suit with pink, teal and purple stripes. She even had sneakers to match.

Neeka looked like she was headed straight for the Olympics.

Genuine champion style.

When we got to the double doors, Ms Parloe was holding them open so kids could walk through.

Neeka stepped forward at the same time I did, her shoulder colliding with mine.

'You can go first,' I said to Neeka.

She looked at me with a sly smirk and asked, 'You know who you look like, right?' I shook my head, knowing without a shadow of doubt I looked like an old church lady.

'Whitley Gilbert!' Neeka chirped smugly.

My cheeks flushed pink.

I loved Whitley as much as anyone else, but she was a girly girl.

The exact opposite of me.

I didn't shoot back at Neeka, though. I took a different tack.

I swallowed the lump in my throat and asked her nicely, 'Jaleesa Vinson or Lena James?'

I figured if I knew who her favourite was, it could tell me something about her.

She laughed mockingly at first, then narrowed her eyes at me in doubt. After a minute, her lips curved into a half-moon smile. 'Lena. Hands down.'

I smiled back. 'Me too. Well, Jaleesa *used to be* my favourite. But not any more.'

She raised her palm. I smacked it good, sealing the deal.

By the time we walked into the auditorium for morning assembly, our arms were slung around each other's shoulders like we'd been friends forever. When Neeka introduced me to Alexis, and we realized that all three of us were deathly allergic to dresses, loved Etonic sneakers and were still rolling with the Kid 'n Play, we decided to sign up for the All City fifth grade track meet.

It took place every year, a few weeks after school started.

At the first practice with Coach Rosse, we met Luce.

That's also when we found out that Neeka was blazing fast.

Alexis, Luce and I were fast too. But not like Neeka.

Coach said Neeka had a superpower. Just like Dama, her sister.

Our last practice that year was at the end of October.

We were getting ready to leave the track when Neeka bent over, pulled her laces tight, folded them in a bow, and said, 'We should keep running after All City.' She pulled her laces tight again. 'We could have our own running squad. That way, next year when team sports start, we'll be ready for track. Since there's four of us, we could even try for the relay.'

I traded glances with Alexis. 'I'm in.'

Alexis looked iffy. 'How often do we run?'

'I don't know,' Neeka said to her. 'We can ask Coach. But if we're gonna do this, we gotta do this.'

'I wanna do it too,' Luce said. 'Let's swear on it.' She flexed her pinkie finger.

'All right,' Alexis said.

I pushed myself out of Momma's chair and stood up looking for some tissue.

I was trying to hold back a second wave of tears from flooding my face, but I wasn't sure how long I could last.

43.
TELL ME A STORY

A few minutes later, I was climbing back up the stairs. Aunt Rose must've read the wreck on my face because I'd barely taken two steps into my bedroom when she rushed over to me. And that's what finally did it. She grabbed my shoulders and rocked me side to side like I was a brand-new baby. When she was done, she lifted the sleeve of her night dress to my nose. 'Take this,' she commanded. She wanted me to use it like a tissue to sop up the snot that was heading past my lip to my chin. 'Go ahead,' she prodded.

I looked at her, with my burning red eyes, and almost sputtered out a laugh.

This was the second time Aunt Rose nearly made me pee my pants with laughter when I was crying. I shook my head no and made my way to my bed, throwing myself over my pillow. Aunt Rose ran over to the desk to get some Kleenex and stuffed a wad in my hand.

She sat down next to me, and dragged me back up.

She hummed a tune I'd never heard before, rocking me side to side.

We sat like that for a while.

Aunt Rose humming and rocking and stopping every now and again to bring me fresh tissue. Eventually, when we had a small mountain of crumbled, wet nastiness at our feet, I asked Aunt Rose to tell me a story.

'Yes, yes!' she said, very eager. 'Of course. What won't bore you?'

I blew into a wet tissue. 'Anything.'

She thought for a minute, then clapped. 'I've got it! I'll tell you about the Ngorongoro Crater, one of the wondrous places of my heart.' Aunt Rose looked at me for approval and I nodded.

She continued. 'Your grandfather, Babu, always said that people travelled thousands of miles across the world to see the wonders at our doorstep. Wonders that we sometimes took for granted. So, he made it a point to take us to as many places in Tanzania with him as he could, whenever his time and his pocket allowed. My favourite place of all was Ngorongoro.'

It sounded like Aunt Rose was excited so I decided to get more comfortable and slipped under my covers. I wasn't even shocked when Aunt Rose lay down and squeezed in next to me. She smiled her ivory-white smile. 'The place is breathtaking, I assure you. A vast land with wildlife, all the animals you can imagine and more. A sky that sweeps blue across the earth with no beginning and no end. There are lush waterfalls and crater lakes and footprints from long ago, when we were becoming humans. And there is the night sky.'

'I guess you really like night skies,' I said remembering her story about the family shamba at Mount Kilimanjaro.

'Oh,' she said, the excitement bubbling up in her voice even more. 'I do. Though they are all cut from the same cloth, this one is even more magical than the rest. When you watch night fall at Ngorongoro, you travel back in time. You can feel it echoing in your ears and all around you. Some nights the sun doesn't set so much as it flames. And once the sky fire dies, when the last embers have quieted, and you think the show is finished, the stars emerge like true ambassadors of light, and you are amazed, once more.'

'Wow,' I said. 'Baba's never said anything like that.'

Aunt Rose chuckled. 'I told you, *kipenzi*. I am much better at this than your father.'

'What else?' I asked, feeling her warmth against me. My twin bed was too small for us, but I didn't care. I just wanted to be lost in her words. Anything to forget everything that had just happened.

'The colours of the place,' Aunt Rose said. 'They defeat the rainbow.'

'Defeat?' I asked, unsure what she meant.

'Let me say, they are better than even a rainbow. The pinks of the flamingos. The greens of the grass shimmering this way and that. Even the white mist cannot be described well with words. It is a living breathing thing. And a feeling. But would you like to know the best part, even better than the mists and the night?'

I nodded my head, yes, and she patted my side.

'The best part is that you can feel the natural beat of life. It is never lost, searching for itself. It is never waiting to start or to finish. It doesn't come and go, depending on rain or shine, visitors or no visitors. It does not come to an end. It is always there. Moving, moving, moving. When you close your eyes at night, you can hear it sounding everywhere, like the heartbeats you loved so much as a child: *badoom, badoom, badoom*. Ngorongoro is a teacher, a healer, a musician, a builder, a record keeper, a creator and more.'

Before the baton drop, I would have probably wanted to know more.

Especially about the rhythm.

Like, could you just stand there and let it fill you up?

Could you take it with you?

I probably would have confessed to Aunt Rose that she had been right, too.

Turns out, she did know me pretty well.

We both kept an eye on rituals, and rhythms and superstition.

But not tonight.

No questions. Only listening.

While I rearranged my body against a hard wall on one side and a soft body on the other, I let Aunt Rose's voice fill my ears with more tales of Ngorongoro and tried to let them transport me to a universe that sounded much better than this one.

A universe where rhythm kept moving.

A universe where it hadn't skidded to a sharp stop.

44.
LAUGHING STOCK OF THE WHOLE SEVENTH GRADE

'But everyone's laughing at me,' I complained the next morning, forgetting all about the magical universe Aunt Rose had built with her words and remembering the present one.

Where I had made a very real fool of myself.

Alexis rolled her eyes. 'Kam. No one is paying you any mind. *Seeeeeee!*' She said it all dramatically as she looked around the hallway. It was just after first period. We were standing by our lockers as a wave of bodies rolled through.

I finished turning the dial of my combination lock. My 'home of all things' (that's what the four of us called our lockers) clicked open. 'Then why was everyone staring at me in math class?' I shoved my math book in and rooted around for my notebook.

Alexis snorted. 'Because you look like the Cookie

Monster.' She raised her hands like claws, looking ridiculous.

'*Huh?*'

'Who knows, Kam? Because you suck at math. But for real, who cares?'

'I care.' I peered one last time in my locker, then slammed it shut. I picked up my backpack from the floor and jammed my notebook in.

'You need to keep it moving. We have the state championship to win next weekend. Care about that.'

Win? I never wanted to hear that word again.

'You weren't the one who messed up in front of the whole seventh grade. I take it back. The whole world.' I swung my backpack up and wrapped the straps over my shoulders.

'The *whole* world was busy with life. Not our little race.'

'*My* whole world saw. And it wasn't some little race.'

'First of all,' Alexis groaned, 'your only-child state of mind is holding you back yet again. If you had siblings, you'd know that moving on is a survival strategy. Otherwise, you'd always be swimming in mad. Second, it was just a *race*. Third, stop being so hectic.' She swung her head around and I was distracted for a moment by her new braids. When I ran my fingers across the wooden beads, they clack, clack, clacked.

I loved that sound.

She must've gotten them done on Sunday. I was glad one of us looked cute.

'*Heeeey*,' Alexis said, smiling slyly and drawing out the syllable. She leaned back against her locker and crossed her arms, lifting her knee and planting a foot on the wall. 'I almost forgot. Have you and Odysseus spoken since the whole Hand Holding Episode?'

I didn't have any good answer for that question.

I still hadn't spoken to Odie.

When we dropped him off at home after the flaming fiasco of a meet, I couldn't meet his eyes. I could barely mumble goodbye.

And even though he'd called once and left a message, I hadn't called him back.

How could I?

I couldn't. And not because I was too embarrassed, which obviously I was.

But because a small part of me was stalling.

Some part of me hoped we weren't former best friends any more.

Maybe deep down, we were *still* best friends.

He *had* grabbed my hand, right? And he had called.

I had already lost his friendship once. I was losing more things by the minute.

I was too scared to find out the truth.

Maybe he was calling to say sorry about the meet, but we still weren't friends.

I didn't need any more disappointments.

'Uhm . . .' I stuttered. 'He's fine, I guess.'

Alexis looked at me wide-eyed. '*You guess*? You actually haven't spoken to him?'

180

I could feel heat rising to my cheeks again. 'What's there to talk about? And why are you stressing me with so many questions?'

Alexis shook her head. 'You have to be kidding me. You know there's plenty to talk about.'

She took her hands and clasped them together to make her point.

'I'm not joking.'

'You're playing, then. Playing like you're Eden from *Santa Barbara*.' She chuckled at herself for a second, even though none of this was funny. I sighed. She looked back at me. 'Either way, you know what this means, don't you?'

'No, actually I don't.'

Alexis cocked an eyebrow.

Just as I was adjusting myself and trying to think of a comeback, I saw Neeka approaching. She stopped dead in front of us, steely eyed, and blinked hard. Like she was trying to blink me away. My body froze up.

Do I say hi?

Do I not say hi?

Do I say sorry?

Do I say nothing?

After last night's call, I settled on nothing.

So did Neeka.

Our eyes locked for a second and then she swivelled her head towards Alexis. Her long black ponytail and her backpack swivelled with her. 'So, I'll see you at lunch?' Neeka asked Alexis, biting off the words. The rims of my ears started burning.

No one spoke for a few seconds.

Alexis stared at Neeka. And then at me.

I shifted my feet.

Alexis put her hand on my shoulder. 'Yes, *we'll* see you at lunch.'

Neeka whirled on us, sigh-stomping away without saying a word.

My stomach clenched as I pulled my backpack straps tighter. 'I guess that's that.'

Alexis put her arm around my shoulder, and we started walking to our next class. 'Don't worry about it. You know how she is.'

I did. That's why I was worried.

The warning bell rang, and we picked up the pace.

I turned my head to Alexis. 'I knew she'd never get over it.'

'Have *you?*' She raised an eyebrow.

'Have I what?'

'Gotten over it?'

'No. She called me a loser, just like Crazy-Cold Eyes. How could I forget that?'

'Well, then there you have it,' Alexis said, smiling and finger-waving at Priya, and then Donovan, and then Levi and then Jen B. As we fought our way around the corner, someone flung their binder in the air. We ducked to avoid getting our own heads clocked. I had no idea why people were so stupid. We kept moving and dodged another unidentified flying object.

Alexis pushed me into our science class.

I scowled at her.

'Just doing my job and keeping you safe,' she said, smiling and brushing off invisible lint from her pants. 'Trust me. You two will work it out. Neeka wants to win more than anything.'

It was true.

Neeka was the only person who wanted to be a state track champion as much as I did. Maybe even *more* than I did.

I knew Neeka, though.

She held grudges.

I didn't see her moving past this anytime soon.

It wasn't in her nature to get over things quick.

Deep down, I knew it wasn't in mine either.

45.
BAD MEDICINE

Neeka was nowhere in sight that afternoon. Not at lunch, and not after school. But Alexis, Luce and I met in the locker rooms before practice and walked over to the track together.

Just hearing the word *track* left a bitter taste on my tongue.

Like bad medicine.

Seeing it was even worse.

I gritted my teeth as we stepped onto the red rubber.

The ground seesawed all over again. A few more steps and we'd be on the grass.

I quickened my pace, leaving Alexis and Luce behind me.

'Where are you rushing to?' Alexis asked, her beads shimmying as she walked.

She and Luce caught up to me.

'Nowhere,' I said, slowing down. 'I just want to get there.'

Ahead of us, on the far end of the track, I could see a circle of girls sitting on the grass. Alexis glanced over at me. 'You *really* have to get over it now.'

I stopped walking and turned to her. 'How would you feel if you were me?'

'I guess I'd feel bad for a minute,' she said, shifting her stance. 'And then, like I said this morning, I'd move on. We lost. *So what?* It's not a permanent situation. We have one more meet.'

Luce squeezed her way in between us. She put one hand on Alexis's shoulder and one hand on mine. 'No fighting.'

I shook myself free from Luce and started walking again. 'Alexis and I aren't fighting. Neeka and I are.'

Once the circle was in full view, we saw that Neeka had already joined.

She was looking surly as we strode up.

Once we got close, her face hardened into a block of ice.

Cold and unmoving.

Alexis marched around the circle and stopped right beside Neeka.

I hung back.

Luce stayed with me. She wouldn't ever leave me in the lurch.

Alexis waved us over so hard I was sure her arm was going to fall off.

When I didn't move, Luce nudged my shoulder with hers. Then she grabbed my hand and pulled me around the circle, stopping right where Alexis was standing.

The exact spot that I wanted to avoid.

Alexis sat down in the grass next to Neeka.

Luce sat down next to Alexis, tugging my arm down with her.

I heard Neeka groan.

Wasn't long before Coach was standing in front of us. Hat cocked. Preaching a whole sermon again.

You had a great meet, and you gave it your all . . .

You were gladiators . . .

And even through the highs and the lows . . .

None of you gave up . . .

We got second place in the team competition, and I know with the same effort, you can take us all the way next Saturday . . .

So . . . let's double down and go get it . . .

I was waiting for him to end with something about the Promised Land.

Instead, he ended with something much worse.

46.
STEP IT UP

Coach wanted to speak with the four of us.

What was next? Was I getting dropped from the relay?

While the rest of our team ran off footloose and fancy free, the four of us sat right where we were with our knees pulled tight into our bodies.

Alexis all smiling.

Neeka all seething.

And Luce all sorry.

As for me, I was bracing for the worst.

'So,' Coach Rosse said, standing tall and serious-like. 'I just wanted to give you a heads up. Because I know some of you don't like surprises.' Whether he was referring to me, or Neeka, or both of us was unclear. 'And because I know how hard the four of you have worked all season long.' I kept my eyes lowered and rubbed my hands up and down my shins to keep warm.

The weather had decided to play cool again.

Not that we needed any more ice the way Neeka was serving it up.

'We're a heavy favourite this year. Even with what happened at the regional meet.' Coach looked at each of us in the eye. 'And your drive and acceleration have improved tremendously this season.'

I nodded.

'But as you know, the 4 x 100 is usually won in the exchange zone. Kam, what happened with the baton could've happened to anyone. You can't let that stop you. Still, I want you all to step it up before the last meet.'

I looked over at Alexis.

One of her eyebrows was raised and she was mouthing something to herself.

I couldn't hear her; I could only imagine what she was saying:

I am one person. How do I keep both Kam and Neeka calm at the same time?

I stole a glance at Neeka.

Her whole face was pure arctic.

'And, specifically,' Coach continued, 'I want you to work more closely with Laina. I know she practised the drills early in the season. But not consistently. I'll let you know when to include her, and I don't want any push-back when I do. Got it?'

Nobody answered.

I think I stopped breathing.

My heart dropped to my feet.

It was cold-blooded Neeka who asked, 'Does this

mean Kam is out and Laina is in?' I turned my whole body over to her this time and stared, clenching my toes inside my sneakers to keep from exploding.

Coach cleared his throat. 'No, Neeka. I just want to make sure we are prepared with an extra runner just in case. We should always have an alternate. We've been short on sprinters who feel comfortable enough with the hundred, but Laina fits the bill now.'

Neeka sat forward and pushed her legs out in front of her. 'All right.'

'Any other questions?' Coach asked. We shook our heads, no.

'OK, run time. Let's go.'

47.
IF ONLY

'She hates me,' I grumbled into my bedsheet, which was pulled up over my head.

Aunt Rose coughed. There was a bit of a rustle on her side of the room. 'Do you mean Daneeka?' I nodded into the sheet. 'She doesn't hate you. She's disappointed. Just like you are.'

My face got warm. 'She wants me taken off the relay. I could tell at practice today.'

Aunt Rose's voice softened. 'Kamaria, I don't think that's true. I think, like you, she mapped out the race in her mind. It didn't go as she expected. Now she's hurt. Can't you see yourself in Daneeka?'

Yes.

I shook my head under the sheet. 'No, I can't.'

'Well, earlier this evening, we spoke about Baba, and I asked you the same thing.'

'I know. I don't see myself in Baba either. That's gross.'

I'd been talking to Aunt Rose in spurts for the better

part of the night, and I tried really hard but I don't think I was actually hearing anything she was saying.

All I could think about was how mad everyone had been at me lately.

First Odie.

I still wasn't ready to face the music and find out why he'd called the night of the track meet. And so far, I'd managed to dodge him at school. He wasn't exactly running over to talk to me, either.

The one time our eyes accidentally met in the hallway, his face turned beet red and I didn't know if it was anger or something else.

Now Neeka.

I pulled the sheet off my head and turned to face Aunt Rose, who wasn't reading her Bible any more. That was her nightly ritual but the book was lying on the bed beside her. I sighed. 'I just want things to be easier. Like . . . right now.'

Aunt Rose gave me a sorry look. She waited a bit like she was trying to gather the right words. 'If only,' she said eventually.

48.
UNASKED AND
UNANSWERED

The next day at school, I went through the rounds with Alexis by my side, but it was Aunt Rose's voice in my ear. She said Neeka was just like me. And I knew she was right.

But then why were we STILL fighting when we wanted the exact same thing?

And how was I supposed to do anything about it?

Especially when we spent our days glowering at each other.

Take today.

We started the day throwing sharp looks at each other . . .

In the hallway . . .

At lunch . . .

By the time we made it to practice, sitting in the grass hinged at our hips and reaching for our toes, Alexis stepped in. 'Can you all stop with the stank faces and speak already?'

Neeka, practically foaming at the mouth, stood up and stormed off.

I rolled my eyes.

Neither of us were budging.

'Ridiculous,' Alexis said eventually, throwing in the towel.

We didn't even talk about the state championship, which was a week and a half away. Normally, Neeka would be bad-mouthing Stasha Mitchell. And we'd be hyping ourselves, talking about how we'd be blasting off like rockets and racking up wins like the Chicago Bulls.

Not this time.

No hype talking.

No grand master planning.

Just anger and the same questions I had in the morning.

Unasked and unanswered.

49.
BABA TERRITORY

'Any progress with Neeka?' Aunt Rose asked the following night. She was sitting cross-legged on the bed with a small pile of towels on her lap and a threaded needle in her hand. She lifted the piece of thread and cut it with her teeth.

'Aunt Rose, I'm sorry. I don't think I'm in the mood to talk tonight.' I watched from my bed as her slim fingers moved swiftly. She was sewing each of our initials onto our towels by hand. The pink pile in her lap was mine. The white ones on top of the dresser were Momma and Baba's. She'd told me a million times already that she'd had monogrammed towels growing up and we should have them, too!

Before Aunt Rose came, I thought I knew the basics of Baba's childhood.

I was slowly learning I was dead wrong.

Aunt Rose looked at me and smiled sympathetically. 'OK, *kipenzi*. If you are too tired tonight, I will talk for both of us. The question to ask yourself is, can you listen?'

I relaxed back into my bed and closed my eyes, thinking about how much I'd talked to Aunt Rose. I was all talked out, but listening I could do. 'Sure.'

'Good. Think of the Ngorongoro nights I've spoken to you about. Covered in a beautiful blanket of darkness. Do you remember what I said about those nights? How they have a sound, a rhythm of their own? Many rhythms, even?'

I nodded, my eyes still closed trying to picture the place as Aunt Rose had described it. I loved the stories about Ngorongoro so much, I'd even asked her to show me the few pictures she brought with her. She didn't have any photos taken at night, though, so right now, I had to rely on the picture she'd drawn with her words.

'I've been thinking about those rhythms,' she said. I popped an eye open for a second and watched the needle and thread still moving in her hands. 'Trying to remember how they sound. How they feel. Trying to get to the root of them. And I realized there was something I forgot to tell you.'

My ears perked and I opened both of my eyes this time, eager to hear something new.

I leaned over to face her.

Aunt Rose's eyes smiled. 'I forgot to tell you that even though the special rhythms of that magical place never stop, they can become disturbed from time to time. They can become jumbled.'

She paused and nodded at me. I nodded back.

She continued. 'When there's a drought, for example, the tracks of the animals change. The water trickles instead of flows. The grass sings less. The rhythms slow. But there is rhythm nonetheless. Sometimes, it moves in the opposite direction. The rhythms quicken when it rains too much. Or when there are too many birds. Rhythm is always there, so long as the place itself is always there. But rhythms change. I wanted you to know this.'

I sighed. I'd had enough of change. It seemed so much had changed, and was changing still. The only thing that hadn't changed was how much I didn't like change.

But then I remembered something. 'What if you still can't hear the rhythm, no matter how hard you try? What if the rhythm falls so out of whack it can't ever come back?'

Aunt Rose paused for a second. 'Those are nice questions. I don't have all the answers, just some more questions. Is that OK?' She smiled a twinkly smile, which I knew was her subtle way of asking if I was ready to talk.

'OK,' I answered, smiling back and saying yes.

'How did you find your chant?'

I blinked, feeling instantly deflated. This wasn't the question I was expecting. If we were moving in this direction, I wasn't sure it was going to help. 'My chant was defective,' I said. 'We didn't win.'

Aunt Rose stuck the needle in the W that she'd almost finished on my towel.

W for Willemina, my middle name.

She set the towel aside. 'That does not answer my question.'

I kicked back the covers, sat up and crossed my legs so that our bodies mirrored one another's. I leaned over and put my chin in my palms. 'I guess I tried to find the right words and the right beats to match us.'

Aunt Rose nodded. 'That is *what* you did. You found the words and the beats, as you call them. But *how* did you do it?'

We were moving into Baba territory now.

I needed a decoder to understand Aunt Rose tonight.

I shrugged my shoulders.

'Think,' Aunt Rose said.

I took a deep breath in. And another. I closed my eyes and tried to think.

Not what, but how.

I thought about all of the lightbulbs that led me to the chant:

The Hawk House chant.

The songs and street sounds that I loved.

The Kiswahili words on Aunt Rose's kanga.

The *click*, *crack*, *boom* of the starting gun.

The cheer of the stands.

My Latin vocabulary words.

Mostly the four of us and what we put into our running.

But that was still the what.

I opened my eyes, the big mess of ideas in my head still

tangled. I sat with them for a few more minutes while Aunt Rose sewed. She patiently looked up at me and then returned to her work.

A minute later, I saw a tiny thread of light behind my eyes pulling me. It pulled and I followed and followed until I sprung up from my bed. 'I tried to listen. I listened. I LISTENED!' I practically screamed the words out.

Aunt Rose nodded and her face grew into the biggest smile I'd ever seen. 'That's exactly it. You quieted, you observed and you listened. There is so much beauty in that. Sometimes we listen to hear and enjoy, which is a wonder. Sometimes we listen to learn and to know. More wonder. There are people that enter Ngorongoro and the sounds echo around them. The rhythm enters their ears. But they do not listen closely. And so, they may hear the *vroom vroom* of the safari vehicle or their own voices or the lion's roar, but nothing deeper. Unless they listen closely, they may miss how all the rhythms come together to tell a story of the land and its people. Still, that is not to say that we all must hear the same thing. But, if there is something we are looking for, we must do the thing many people find it difficult to do. We must keep quiet and listen. And, more importantly, just as Ngorongoro always hears itself, we must strive to do the same. To hear what is around us is very, very important. To hear what is inside us, maybe more so.'

I sat there in silence, really trying to but not sure I understood everything Aunt Rose was saying.

50.
HEARTSONGS

'Another question,' Aunt Rose jumped in, way before I was ready to move on. 'Why was it you to write the chant among all your friends?'

'*Hmmmm*,' I said, tilting my head back. 'Well, besides the fact that it was my idea . . . maybe because I like sounds and words.'

When I lifted my head, Aunt Rose was smiling again.

'Which is to say that you like to listen.'

'I never thought about it that way, I guess. But, yes I think I do. I love listening to music, too.'

'And because you like to listen, you may hear things others don't. It's a gift. I think that the girls know this.'

'But how does listening help when the chant didn't work and we didn't win?'

Aunt Rose chuckled deeply.

A low growl of a chuckle. It was different than her normal laugh. Heavier.

'*What?*' I whined. 'Why are you laughing at me?'

199

'I'm not laughing at you. I'm laughing with you.'

'But I'm not laughing.'

'Your older self is laughing. I'm laughing with her.'

My shoulders slumped. 'What exactly are you saying, Aunt Rose?'

'We were not talking about winning or things working out our way. Those are nice, but they come and go. We were talking about listening. We were talking about listening so deeply we could start to hear and see and feel the connections around us. *That* is what is important to your question. The question you asked about what happens when one feels they've lost their rhythm.'

She was quiet for a moment before she continued. 'Or as I would put it, what happens when you can't hear your own heartsong.'

I looked at her quizzically. 'Heartsong?'

'Yes, yes,' she continued. 'Think of it this way. If you are looking to find the beat that leads to the truth of you, or the rhythm that simply is you, just remember what I said about Ngorongoro. The beat, the rhythm, the song, whatever name you call it, it never dies so long as you are alive. It is always there. And by there, I mean . . .' Aunt Rose stood up and walked over to me. She pointed to my chest. 'Here. Even if you can't hear it and you think you've lost it, it is there.'

She squeezed my side and continued. 'And you are lucky. It seems even when you were small, just a *mtoto*, you were always trying to listen for heartsongs. Anywhere and everywhere.'

'But what about Neeka?' I asked. 'We are completely out of sync and out of rhythm. I can't listen if she won't talk to me. It's out of my control now.'

Aunt Rose smiled shrewdly. 'I think the same – I will use Baba's word now – the same principles apply. Start at the same place. Yes, you have your own personal heart-song. But you are right. You also share heartsongs with others. Especially with dear friends. This is where we can make such beautiful music together. Like you and your sisters zooming around the circle. A beautiful song. So much more than winning or losing. Don't you agree?'

Aunt Rose looked at me. She must've sensed that my eyes were getting heavy.

The sound of her voice was so relaxing, it almost put me to sleep.

I yawned, climbing back under my covers. 'I guess so. But what do I do?'

She went back to her bed and took a minute to put her sewing project away and she got ready for the night, too. 'When you fall out of the circle, you quiet yourself. You start to hunt for the beat that leads to the truth of your sisterhood. You listen closely, following the small notes, feeling the connections, until you can hear the rhythm and then the entire beautiful song, again.'

'OK,' I said, feeling my whole body becoming heavy now. 'I hope so.'

I was almost in dreamland.

But I was still trying to hang on to her every word.

51.
RIDICULOUS AND COMPANY

It was Friday, and by the time Coach whacked his cap against his hand to signal the end of practice, I was already standing up and raring to go.

I was ready to follow the notes chiming in my ear.

I just hoped I'd heard them right.

And had listened enough.

I'd spent the whole morning replaying things in my mind, over and over again.

When it came to track, Neeka and I were the same.

We both loved the 4 x 100 relay.

And we both thought it was the best race in track history!

When it worked out right and the passes were smooth and we gave it all we got, we were like four pairs of feet floating on air.

All of us connected.

A four-part harmony.

And the song went like this:

Alexis had to get us started on the right note.

Luce and I had to keep things steady and keep what Alexis gave us in motion.

Neeka had the hardest job.

She had to take everything we'd gathered – all that running and rhythm – and take it and us across the finish line.

She had to complete the circle.

She had to finish the song.

And she took every step seriously.

Just like I did when I was pushing so hard for a winning chant.

So I figured that even if it was hard to see, Neeka wasn't being heartless right now. She was mad because she was the *exact* opposite of heartless.

She cared so much, just like me.

Maybe Aunt Rose was right.

Maybe both of us weren't just upset about losing.

Maybe it was more than that.

I was still trying to find my own rhythm again.

My heartsong as Aunt Rose called it.

There was still a lot of static in the way.

But after talking with Aunt Rose, I knew I could still hear my song with the girls.

I knew it through and through.

It was everything I wrote in the chant, even if it didn't work and we didn't win.

It was all the things inside of us – in our hearts and our heads and our souls – that brought us together.

Sometimes that sounded like *click*, *crack*, *boom*.

Sometimes it was a *whoosh!*

Other times it was laughter like *aheeheeeheeee!*

Usually, it was just a plain old two-beat pattern – one-two, one-two, one-two.

The sound of us, keeping in pace, side by side when we walked to the Wawa.

We even made people walk around us so we could stay in formation.

Our heartsong, our rhythm, was all of that and more.

It was everything we shared.

'You ready?' I asked Luce, who was still laid out on her back in the grass. She groaned, before pulling up the bottom of her Minnie Mouse T-shirt and using it to wipe the line of sweat dripping down from her hairline into her ear.

Alexis was on the other side of the grass with Neeka.

'Where you rushing to now?' Luce asked, sitting up and squinting at me.

The sun had been playing peek-a-boo, but the clouds were clearing now.

Orange beams danced right into Luce's eyes and around her spirals, which were still perfect ringlets even after our sweat fest.

I moved closer and pulled one of them and it sprang right back.

'I want to talk to Neeka,' I said, giving Luce my hand.

She grabbed it and I pulled her up.

'Well, shoot,' she said, shaking out her legs. 'That's all you had to say. We've been waiting on you two to end the beef. You guys are worse than LL and Kool Moe Dee.'

Before I even had a chance to get to them, I spotted Alexis coming over with Neeka in tow.

I was ready.

When they stopped in front of us, I didn't waste any time. 'I'm really sorry I called you a loud mouth,' I spat out quickly. 'I was just mad at you for being so doggone mean. But I was madder at myself for letting us down.'

Alexis grinned like a Cheshire cat. She and Luce swivelled their heads to Neeka.

Neeka shifted her gaze down. 'I'm sorry too. My bad.'

Alexis and Luce swivelled their heads back to me, waiting for my response.

'Good,' I said, breaking out a small smile.

Neeka and I stood in silence, not knowing what was next.

'Well, that was easy,' Alexis said, lifting her hands to the crown of her head and patting an itchy spot. 'Now, can you two wrap this up?'

'I second that emotion,' Luce crooned.

'OK, Smokey Robinson and the Miracles,' Neeka said.

Luce looked from me to Neeka. 'This is the miracle right here.'

'No more throwing daggers,' I said. 'Promise.'

Alexis sucked her teeth, unsatisfied.

Neeka pulled me in for a hug. 'This is what she wants. Here's your kumbaya.'

Neeka squeezed me and then turned me around by the shoulders, her nose wrinkling. 'By the way, I noticed this raggedy mess all week.' She pulled at an errant braid falling out from my ponytail. My roots were a gigantic puff cloud. 'You're on Struggle Street right here. You need to make a U-turn. And since when do you say doggone?'

I sighed. 'Neeka, don't even . . .'

'*Neeka, don't even*,' she mimicked in a syrupy voice, grinning hard. 'Seriously. You might want to do your hair between now and the state meet. On the *off chance* we get our picture in the paper, you don't wanna be looking dusty. And stop saying doggone while you're at it.'

Alexis twisted her face. 'You two went from throwing flames at each other one minute to talking about having your sweet little picture in the paper in the next to talking about euphemisms for goddamn?' She pulled Neeka by the hand and sighed. She turned to me. 'Ridiculous and company, let's go . . .'

Neeka and I looked at each other with a secret smile, knowing that Alexis using vocabulary that none of us understood was the most ridiculous thing of all.

We kept on walking.

And our rhythm, our heartsong, kept on vibrating throughout my entire being.

52.
THE PLAY-BY-PLAY

In our bedroom that night, I gave Aunt Rose the play-by-play.

She'd already changed into her cotton nightgown.

The one I'd almost used as a handkerchief.

She was putting a silk scarf on her head.

A small hole was starting to work its way bigger on one side of the fabric.

I watched as she pulled the scarf ends all the way around, carefully covering the hole and tying a knot in the back.

Then I started from the beginning.

When I was done, Aunt Rose congratulated me.

'It's crazy,' I said, as I stuck the sharp end of a rattail comb through a braid. 'Once I focused, I was able to see where Neeka was coming from. And then I barely had to listen for our song. It was right there. And when she started on my hair, I was like, yup, we're back.' I picked my way through the braid and it started to unravel. Even though Neeka's razzing me again sounded like music to my ears – back-and-forth roasting was *definitely* part of our rhythm – I was still tired of listening to her talk about how my hair lived on Struggle Street.

'You found a way to let your heart listen,' Aunt Rose said, reaching for her Bible. She opened a dog-eared page and used her finger to hold the place. She looked up at me from the bed. 'You'll have to listen time and time again. But it gets easier.'

I sighed, reaching for the last braid and knowing deep down she was right.

Knowing she'd been right all along.

In just the short time she'd been with us, Aunt Rose had given me enough advice to last a lifetime.

I put the comb down on the bedside table and pumped a little lotion into my hands, smoothing it into my elbows until all the ashy was gone.

It called up a memory:

Aunt Rose using my Vaseline without asking that first night together.

Which felt like a century ago.

Why had that made me so mad?

Aunt Rose sniffed the air and inhaled. 'You smell nice. The lotions here are much nicer than at home.'

I smiled. That was something that had never crossed my mind. Although now that she mentioned it, I remembered that Momma would always send back about five or six bottles of perfume as gifts any time a friend of the family was travelling to Tanzania. 'Your aunties will love these,' she'd always say.

I reached my arms behind me and scooted all the way back. Then I crossed my legs. 'What else is nicer here?'

She plumped her pillow and lay all the way down, spreading her Bible, spine up, across her chest. 'Hmm, let me see.' She put her hands behind her head and pressed one foot on top of the other. 'I like the order of the streets. In Dar, you could easily get run down at any minute. Pedestrians walk in peril.'

'*Really?*' I asked.

'Oh yes,' she smiled.

Crossing the road made me think about Aunt Rose's children.

My cousins.

Saayande was eleven. Two years younger than me.

Aunt Rose said we'd get along fabulously.

She'd inherited the Kessy-neat-except-in-the-kitchen gene, like I did.

She was slow to warm. She liked sports, too.

The twins, Yaro and Tumo, were eight. Fast-talking and full of energy, she said.

I cleared my throat. 'Can I ask you something else?'

'Anything.'

'Was it hard to leave my cousins? I mean, don't they need you for stuff?'

Aunt Rose sat up on her elbows. 'They need me, yes. But others, too. That's something that may be nicer about home. Family everywhere. I have so many people I can count on to help me. But of course, I do miss them.'

I drew in a deep breath. 'Is it hard to be here with us, then?'

Aunt Rose smiled. 'It's easy to be here with you. But it's hard to be away. Both at the same time. But isn't that what this is all about?' She lifted one elbow and waved her hand around. 'We're always learning to balance many things at the same time.'

'I guess so,' I answered, unsure.

'Yes,' Aunt Rose said, like she was reading my uncertainty. 'You, especially.'

'*Me?*'

She nodded. 'You're a dreamer and a thinker. You are black and you are white. You are American and you are Tanzanian.' She settled into bed, looking quiet and content and leaving me to think about her words.

I guess I'd never really thought about it like that before. That balancing the different parts of myself was something I was actually doing.

But the more I thought about it, the more it kind of made sense.

My Tanzanian side, which I was getting to know better thanks to Aunt Rose, and my American side were very different. Different in a good way.

And then I felt a stabbing reminder in my chest of what wasn't balanced.

Odie.

53.
SLOWLY
SLOWLY

I reached over to switch off my lamp, a sweet-and-sour taste coating my mouth.

Aunt Rose was still quiet, so I took a minute to think about Odie.

Our out-of-rhythmness was always there in the back of my mind.

I'd just been able to bury it deep down further while I was working things out with Neeka. Now here it was, creeping back up.

What would our heartsong sound like now, if I could hear it?

Even if I got really quiet, I don't think I'd be able to know.

Maybe I'd ask Aunt Rose for help sometime.

Aunt Rose, unusually quiet, switched her lamp off too.

Moonlight poured in through the window.

We tucked ourselves under the covers at the same time.

Once Aunt Rose heard me yawning, she started in her lullaby voice. 'Tonight, I'll tell you about the home we grew up in. The one in Oyster Bay. Is that fine?'

I could hear the shushing sound of her scarf across the pillowcase.

It reminded me of Momma and Baba's soft whispering sounds.

Shush-shush-shush.

The sound of Momma and Baba's thick love.

'Yup,' I said, smiling thinking of the two of them.

'Good,' Aunt Rose said. 'I've been saving this one.'

I leaned up on my elbows, curious. 'Why?' Even though I'd learned by listening to Aunt Rose that she liked to reveal things at certain times. When she first came a few weeks ago, she started with the oldest stories she could remember. The ones told to her when she was little. Sometimes, she'd throw in a few from her life now. Usually, though, her stories were set way back in the day. Listening to Aunt Rose tell stories was like watching a house being built from the foundation up. She liked to take her time with it, setting things right and patiently waiting for them to settle before moving on to the next brick.

'*Pole, pole*,' she always said about how she liked to tell stories.

Slowly, slowly.

'I was saving it,' she said. 'Because it reminds me of everything good about home. I wanted your spirit to

212

be a bit more settled when I told it to you. That way you could really hear it, through your ears, but mostly I wanted you to hear with your heart. Maybe you'll find pieces of yourself in it, too.'

'OK,' I said.

'OK,' Aunt Rose echoed. I couldn't see her but I could hear the smile in her voice. 'There was a huge, bright pink – I think you call it hot pink,' she chuckled softly to herself, 'bougainvillea in front of the house. In fact, it's the one you see in the picture of Mama and Baba on their wedding day. On that day, the gardener hadn't yet—'

'*Hold on?*' I said into the silvery, shadowy dark, interrupting her for a very good reason. 'You had a *gardener?*'

'We did.'

'Baba always said money was scarce. How could you afford a gardener?'

'Well, money was scarce because we were many. A good amount of money came in. You remember that your Bibi was a civil servant and the first Tanzanian geologist to earn a degree from this very America. But almost all of the money he made went out. Money was merely a visitor. Our family had many responsibilities. And many people to help. But of course we still had people tending the compound.'

Compound?

Holy moly smackaroo!

Baba grew up living large. He thought he was slick, only giving me the bare-bones version of his life growing up in Tanzania. Well, here I was getting the full story and then some because Aunt Rose loved the nitty gritty details.

Aunt Rose couldn't see my eyes bulging out of my head, but they were. 'I've only seen pictures of a nice house with a big yard,' I said. 'Baba never called it a compound. What else was there?'

'Oh,' she continued. 'The pictures can't capture the beauty of the place. We called it a compound because it was behind a gate and there were many people living there. There still are. But your Baba wouldn't have taken many pictures of the acacia trees, or the boys' quarters, or the small house for the *dadas*. You remember Dada Regina, the one who coddled us when we were little?'

'Yup,' I said, easing back down into bed and thinking of Dada Regina's gap-toothed smile and the heart shaped scar on her cheek and the softness of the palms of her hands. I was pretty good at remembering the cast of characters because of the way Aunt Rose described them.

Kiswahili words were easier to hold in my mouth now, too.

'Good,' Aunt Rose said. 'Back to our lovely family compound in Oyster Bay . . .'

I pulled the covers up to my chin and listened to Aunt Rose paint pictures with her words until my eyes slowly blinked shut.

54.
SAY EVERYTHING

Before dinner on Sunday, I called Aunt Rose upstairs for a very important meeting.

She followed me into the bedroom.

When I closed the door behind me, she looked at me very solemnly. 'Is everything OK, Kamaria. You seem too serious.'

I walked into the middle of the room. 'Please take a seat.'

She moved over to the desk but I pointed to the bed. 'Get comfy.'

'OK,' she said, sitting down and placing her hands softly on her lap.

I sat down on the edge of my bed, my hands on my knees. 'I'd like to ask your advice.'

She breathed out and placed her hand on her heart. 'My goodness, is that all? You scared me. We talk every night, no?'

I nodded. 'Yes, but this is different. This is about Odie.'

215

She smiled curiously. 'Ah, yes. Odysseus. In the car ride to the track meeting . . .'

I nearly busted out laughing.

Aunt Rose was so Luce with the way she said things.

'What?' she asked innocently.

'Nothing. You were saying about Odie . . . On the way to the track *meeting* . . .'

'Yes, on the way to the meeting, I sat in the back of the car with Odysseus, and we talked and we talked. And I could tell by the way he spoke about you that he was . . . how can I say . . . a very special friend.'

I nodded.

I'd never spoken to Aunt Rose about Odie.

It all came out in a huge rush.

How we used to play in the mud ages ago and how we played CDs up until a few months ago. How we had never really hit any bumps in the road in all thirteen years of our friendship because we got one another. How he kind of knew me better than I knew myself and could always get me out of a funk and back on track. And how our rhythm was such a part of my life that I didn't even feel like myself without it.

I just kept going, while Aunt Rose sat quiet, perched on the side of the bed, listening. I even confessed my fears about her coming and taking up Odie's seat at the kitchen table. I told her that I didn't balance things as well as she thought I did because something about eating lunch with the girls in February had erased our friendship.

That's how we ended up here.

Not speaking.

When I explained that Odie holding my hand was the first chink of light I'd seen in our friendship in months, Aunt Rose asked, 'But doesn't that give you hope?'

'Kind of, but not really,' I said, taking a breath after I'd spilled my guts. 'I'm afraid that maybe it wasn't a light. Maybe it was more like a mirage. Or a hand-out. Literally. Maybe he held my hand because he felt sorry for me, but he still doesn't want my friendship back.'

Aunt Rose shook her head in disagreement.

But I barrelled on, 'And you know what else?'

'What?' Aunt Rose asked with so much warmth in her voice.

I climbed down from the bed and sat on the floor, binding my arms around my knees. 'You know how I was able to say sorry to Neeka and we found our rhythm again all in one shot?'

She nodded.

'I don't think that will work with Odie. I've tried following the trail and listening for the soft notes. All I can hear is scratching, like my TLC CD.'

Aunt Rose looked at me puzzled. 'What do you mean?'

'My TLC CD is my favourite one. But I listened to it so much I scratched it. If I try to play it now, all of the good parts are still there. But when the scratch comes around it skips and sounds horrible. It's ruined. One tiny scratch and the whole CD is trash. That's what happened to us. One scratch and our friendship was ruined. Our heartsong is scratched up, too . . .'

Aunt Rose breathed in deeply. '*Subiri*,' she said, standing up. 'Just one minute.' She went and got something from the neat stack on her side of the closet. She came back over to me with a piece of cloth and opened it.

'Another kanga?' I asked.

She nodded. 'This is even simpler than the last one. Also, beautiful.'

She sat crouched down next to me on the carpet and laid it over me. The kanga was baby blue, my favourite colour, and very plainly designed with white lines and circles. '*Sema yote?*' I said, reading the two words at the bottom of the kanga slowly.

She raised and dropped her eyebrows quickly, which was her way of saying yes.

Just like Baba.

'*Sema yote* means, "say everything".'

I nodded. 'Nice design.'

'Kangas weren't only for wearing, you know. Before, they could be used to send messages, too.'

'Really?'

'Yes. If a woman wanted to tell her neighbour something, she might wear a kanga to deliver the message instead of confronting her directly.'

'So, someone could wear this one and she would be telling her neighbour to say everything?'

A glint sharpened Aunt Rose's eye. 'Maybe. Or maybe the neighbour did something hurtful, and she might want to discuss it. So, she wears the *sema yote* kanga to tell her friend that they have to get things out on the table. It can mean many things. It depends. But since you've called me here to tell me everything. I know it's a sign.'

I nodded slowly. 'But saying everything to you and saying everything to Odie is a totally different story.'

'How so?' Aunt Rose asked.

'I can come to you with everything all mixed up and lots of questions. I feel like I need to know everything I did wrong, have it all figured out, before I can say anything to Odie.'

'You don't have to know it all.' She patted my arm. 'You can't. That's impossible. But you can say everything that is in your heart. And you have practice. You started with Neeka.'

'That wasn't the same. I apologized in two seconds and she punched me in the arm and I pushed her back and she made fun of my hair and it was done. Odie and I haven't talked in months. It's kind of deeper, I guess.'

'I am sure you will be fine.'

I scooted back and pulled the kanga around me. 'But what if I'm not?'

She gave me a look so sorry, it looked like the sorry was filling her up. 'It's true that sometimes relationships bend so far, they break. But you will never know until you try.'

That wasn't what I wanted to hear.

It was my worst fear. Even worse than losing the relay.

I sat with it for a second.

Then, I looked up at Aunt Rose and her sad-sorry face and realized maybe she wasn't just talking about me. Maybe she was talking about her rolling stone of a husband who fell off the face of the earth. I glanced down, feeling so bad, but when I looked back up, her face had rearranged itself.

I felt confused and relieved and sad and sorry all at the same time.

It was strange to see Aunt Rose's face look like anything but the bright sun it always was, even though it was just for a second. I promised myself that the next time I saw a look like that cross her face, I would ask her about it.

When Aunt Rose stood up a moment later, her true twinkle had returned. 'Time for me to start dinner. My favourite part of the day.'

'Can I help you?' I asked, staring up at her, even though I detested cooking.

'Oh no. You have plenty of work to do right here. Gather your courage. Think about what you want to say to Odie so that when the time comes, you're ready.'

She winked at me and then walked out of the room.

55.
STATIC

'Dinner was out-of-this-world delicious, Rose,' Momma said a few hours later. She folded her legs up on the couch and her bare feet pressed into my thigh.

Aunt Rose's eyes were still twinkling. 'You see. And no animal was sacrificed. I can cook without meat, too.' The four of us were sitting in the living room after dinner, waiting for Baba to find something we could all watch.

He clicked and clicked the remote but, as usual, saw nothing he liked.

'It really was yum. Thank you, Aunt Rose,' I added, with a smile.

'Please don't thank,' she said, swatting her hand at me. She was sitting in the armchair across from the couch. She crossed her arms and then sat back even further, looking very satisfied. 'Cooking for you is a joy.'

'Well, you're much, much better at it than I am,' Momma said, smiling. 'I think we can all agree.' She looked around at all of us for agreement.

Baba coughed and kept fiddling with the remote.

Aunt Rose nodded her head knowingly, unafraid of the plain truth.

I shrugged.

'I almost forgot,' Momma said, reaching over to me and smoothing down a runaway curl that was bouncing out of my head. 'I told Aunt Rose this morning, but you were nowhere to be seen so I didn't get a chance to tell you. Aunt Darien is coming over soon. She's been so busy with her nursing shifts that she still hasn't met Aunt Rose.'

I ran my thumbs across the seams of my jeans.

And then it struck me!

That's why Aunt Rose had winked at the end of our conversation. She knew Aunt Darien was coming.

Maybe there was a chance Odie was coming, too.

On the TV, the new soda commercial I loved started playing.

The one with En Vogue singing.

But I was too nervous to hear it.

All I could make out was the sound of static crackling in my head.

Aunt Darien reached her arms out and squeezed me tight when I opened the front door. 'Kam, I miss you. I haven't seen you in ages.'

I smiled. 'Not *ages*.'

She took my chin in her hand. 'Seems that way. When was the last time we had a long chat? Just the two of us?'

I shrugged. She let my face go and walked into the front hall, taking off her jacket and shoes and tucking them away like it was second nature.

I craned my neck to look behind her. 'Is Odie with you?'

She shook her head, linking her arm in mine. 'He's at home, hun. He said since he'd already met Aunt Rose, he'd leave me to it. Plus, he wanted to get his new music in order.'

I nodded and forced a smile as Momma came in under the archway shooing us in. I stood around twiddling my thumbs for a whole ten minutes before I asked Momma and Baba if I could run over to Odie's. They were too busy chatting to give me any grief and barely looked up when I asked them, but Aunt Rose smiled her sunshine smile at me and it was all I needed. I could hear her cotton-candy sweetness wrapping around Aunt Darien while I tied my laces.

Then I drew in a breath from deep, deep down and took off.

56.
SCARED-STUCK

I didn't shake the broken handle on the side-screen door and just let myself in like I used to. I waited a second, standing on Odie's stoop and looking up at his window.

The blinds were open.

I took a deep breath and pressed the doorbell, then clasped my hands in front of me.

Nothing.

I rang the bell again and waited.

Still no answer.

I started to worry that Odie wasn't home.

Maybe he'd left and I'd gathered every ounce of courage I had for nothing.

I must've waited five more minutes before I started to back up – my heels moving slowly down the stairs in reverse.

Next thing I knew the front door swung open.

Odie walked out and crossed his arms with an unreadable face. 'What's up?'

A thick silence mixed with dread hung over me.

Odie coughed.

'Can I please come in?' I asked, trying to ignore the heat creeping from the tips of my toes all the way up.

Odie was holding a few CDs in his hand.

He didn't say anything, he just turned around, stepping back into the house.

He glanced at me sideways like he was waiting for something.

'Actually,' I said in a serious voice and picturing the *sema yote* kanga folded in a small square on top of my pillow. I took another deep-down breath. 'I wanted to talk to you about something.'

'Fine,' he said, walking upstairs.

I stood behind Odie, watching him drop the clutch of CDs on his bed and feeling relieved I was still 'allowed' in his room.

When he turned around, we were standing face to face.

I tried to swallow but couldn't.

I had that strange feeling again.

The one I had when Baba first told me Aunt Rose was coming.

Like there wasn't enough air in the room for both of us to breathe.

But this time, I knew what to do.

I'd been looking at and listening to everything around me and inside me and I could sense that the air was just a little lighter and the tone in Odie's voice was a smidge less spiky and even though my heart was beating faster than it did on race day, I swear I thought I could hear something coming in.

Say everything.

The words echoed inside of me.

I looked down at my feet, then lifted my eyes. 'I'm sorry, Odie.'

Odie sat down on the floor and leaned his head back against the side of his bed. He nodded, looking up at me and keeping his eyes on mine.

'I don't know exactly what I did,' I continued. 'But I know when I started eating lunch with the girls, our friendship kind of took a left turn. I don't know if it's because our routine changed, or we didn't talk about it. I asked you if you wanted to eat with us and when you said no, I figured you didn't care.' I sat down next to him. Close enough to feel his leg twitching and the goosebumps on his bare arm instantly rise up.

He sat forward and ran his fingers through his hair, moving it off his face.

He tilted his head towards me. 'Why wouldn't I care? We're best friends, aren't we? What would you do if I suddenly asked you to eat with me and the Halsey twins?'

I made a face. 'I'd vomit. They don't eat. They inhale food through their nostrils.'

He doubled over and pretended to barf and then climbed up onto his bed with what I thought might be a crack of a smile. 'No offence, but you thought I'd want to eat with you guys? When you and Alexis are together, you don't talk. You shriek. Or you speak in slanguage or whatever.'

'*Wait*,' I said. 'Alexis and I do *not* shriek!'

Yeah. Maybe sometimes we squealed.

He shrugged, making a serious face now. 'And even though you asked me to eat with you guys, you were bouncing on your tippy toes and squinting your eyes, which is a tell-tale sign. It means when you ask a question, you hope the answer is no.'

'That's not—'

Odie raised his right eyebrow.

My eye twitched. 'Even if I did, it's not what I meant, Odie. I swear.'

'Well, it felt that way. Like you were pushing me aside. You never explained why. And then you never said sorry. Everything felt different after that.'

I nodded.

He continued. 'You know I don't have a ton of friends like you do. I guess I felt replaceable. Simple really.' He paused for a few beats. 'So why has it taken you so long?'

'Because I'm dense?' I said slowly, raising my shoulders and feeling the weight of my mistake. Never in a million years did I think Odie could feel replaced.

Or that he thought I didn't truly want him to eat with us when I did.

He nodded. 'You said it not me.'

I walloped his leg and then scooted closer to the bed. 'Honestly, Odie. I wasn't trying to replace you. I didn't think you'd really care if I ate with the girls.' I pressed my feet into the soft carpet and hugged my knees. 'And then I thought you were being pig-headed to not eat with us.' I sighed. 'And then you were so mad, I think I just got scared-stuck. And then at the track meet . . .'

The words trailed off.

The tips of my ears burned and I couldn't get any more out.

Maybe it wasn't everything. But it was enough.

Odie's face stared down at me from the bed for what felt like a really long time. Then it softened. 'Next time, just ask.'

'Point taken. I'll try to.'

A few more slow seconds passed.

'So, how's it going?' he asked, reaching his hand behind his back and grabbing a few CDs. He started arranging them in the order he wanted them played.

I went to grab the portable CD player from Odie's desk just like I used to, hoping and praying he wouldn't stop me or say he'd had enough and I had to go home.

Hoping and praying we could stay in this rhythm.

'You mean with Aunt Rose? Or, with track. Or . . .?'

'Yup,' he said.

I sat back down, placing the player on the floor. 'As far as Aunt Rose goes, we have your mom over,' I checked my watch, 'at 6:30 p.m. on Sunday and you know how Baba feels about Sundays and preparing for the week, so that says something. Now that Aunt Rose is here, Baba's all footloose and fancy free.'

228

Odie laughed. He gently tossed me the first case from his pile.

I pulled the CD out and pressed it down hard into the player in front of us.

'Easy does it, Kam,' he said.

I rolled my eyes and hit play. 'For the millionth time,' I said, lifting my eyes to look at him. 'I got this.'

Odie raised an eyebrow. 'Really? That's why all your CDs are scratched.'

I ignored him and his rightness. 'Anyway. You saw Aunt Rose. She's like the sun come to life.' I turned the volume down. 'It's been kinda fun to be honest.'

'Yeah, well, she seems cool.' Odie climbed down from the bed and sat next to me on the carpet. He turned the volume back up and I wondered what he and Aunt Rose talked about on the one-hour ride to the regional meet.

'Did you notice we kind of look alike?'

'I didn't look at her *that* closely,' he said, smiling.

'Well, we do. It threw me off at first, but it's actually kind of nice to look like a family member who's not Baba.' Odie nodded and chuckled, and I could feel us slowly getting unstuck. Slipping back into our familiar flow – fast streams of words and slow stretches of comfortable silence.

We both sat quietly for a while listening to the steady *thump*, *thump*, *thump*, until Odie said, 'Are you feeling ready for the state meet after the . . . Well . . . When is it exactly?'

As if on cue, the CD skipped.

We both reached for the CD player.

Our hands crashed into one another.

'It's in a week and a half,' I said, my heart beating fast.

He scooted back a few inches. 'Cool. I'm sure it'll be better.'

I gripped the carpet with my toes. 'Maybe.'

'*Maybe?*' he said, cocking his head. His hair tumbled into his face. He did his nod thing. 'Definitely.'

I shrugged.

Odie grinned. 'Chili time.'

'Fine!' I said, snapping back. He handed me the CD and I swapped it out and we listened to the Red Hot Chili Peppers screaming about giving things away to their mamas and their papas all the way through and I didn't complain once. After listening to two more albums from start to finish, I noticed the time and realized I was pushing my luck and better head home. We let the last song play out and both agreed that it was the best song we'd heard all night. The way Arrested Development sang out about everyday people was our favourite part. It was really different from the way Sly and the Family Stone sang the same words in a different song that we both loved from *way* back when.

But it was also familiar.

Which was weird because, suddenly, that's how things felt with Odie.

Really different and really familiar.

I knew exactly what Alexis was going to ask me when

I snuck in a phone call later that night: 'So, Kam, is the Great Mystery Episode finally over?'

The strange thing was, I didn't know.

Odie and I had gone over a lot.

Almost everything . . .

But not holding hands.

I still couldn't ask him about that.

PART THREE:

GO

57.
TING-A-LING-LING-LINGS

The entire girls' track team sat on the wet, rubbery track on Monday, praying for practice to be cancelled. The rain had stopped a few hours ago, but grey cottony clouds still stretched across the sky, threatening to empty themselves right on our heads.

Coach Rosse was oblivious.

He didn't care about rain, sleet, snow or shine.

He always found a way to keep practice going.

While he motored on through his pep talk, I heard other things.

Luce and Alexis snickering next to me.

And even though Neeka was sitting across the way, I could hear a part of her, too. The part of her that was tuned to me, now that we'd found our flow again.

It had only been a few days, but Odie and I were inching back, too.

We even sat together in science class today.

When Mr Dobalina started asking again about our

Night of Learning projects, I slipped Odie a note that read: *HELP?!?!?* and he gave me a thumbs up.

Everything that had been wrong was starting to right itself.

It felt good. But still not good enough to erase all my doubts.

I'd been getting some ting-a-ling-ling-lings, but I was still feeling unsure about my rhythm. Part of me thought it would rush back and I'd hear it crystal clear when Neeka and I made up. I was sure once everything with Odie was better, I would definitely find my own rhythm and flow, again.

But every time I stepped on the track, a small part of me still felt unsteady.

Out of step.

Wibbly wobbly.

I was waiting, listening for the familiar tones and turns and wondering why it was taking so long for my rhythm to come back. I was praying like crazy it would make its way back before the state championship on Saturday.

I caught the tail end of Coach Rosse talking.

When I heard him announce, 'Park run today, girls,' I bolted upright, and wiped off my wet shorts, while the girls carried on moaning and groaning.

I was happy to get off the track.

Maybe a long run could help me find my stride.

We started just past the playground and ran down Boxer's Trail.

By the time we reached Rockland, I could breathe out

all the knots in my stomach. Once we turned the corner with Laurel Hill in front of us, I took the wind until Strawberry Mansion and then I coasted.

My feet did all the thinking.

The rest of me just glided.

It was actually working.

I *finally* felt at home.

Part of the great nothing and everything.

It was perfect . . . until the end of practice.

'Relay teams, can I have a word?' Coach called out when he was finished with his closing sermon for the day. 'Laina and Cherisse, you too.'

My chest tightened.

Luce felt a little shaky next to me as I leaned on her shoulder to stand up.

I bounced on my toes, looking around at the ten of us and ignoring the burn in my muscles. Coach had called together our 4 x 100 relay team, the other four girls for the sprint medley relay team, and the two alternates.

Laina was ours. Cherisse was the other team's.

'This is our last week of practice,' Coach Rosse said. 'And like I mentioned to each of your relay teams before, we need to practise with the alternates so we can make sure everybody's up to speed.' He chuckled. 'Did you see what I did there? Speed? Runners?'

Coach could get corny with the track jokes quick.

We rolled our eyes. This was no time to joke.

He thwacked his hat against his hand. 'Anyway, all understood?'

'Yup,' Neeka said, too confidently and too quickly.

The rest of us mumbled agreement.

'Good,' Coach said, rubbing the back of his hatless head. His hair was freshly cut and dusted with grey. 'Laina, you know you'll be with the 4 x 100 and Cherisse with the medley. You all have practised this before so I expect it will be smooth sailing. You'll start tomorrow. Any last questions? Let's get 'em out now.'

'Nope,' Neeka said, wearing a blank face.

It didn't sound smooth to me, but I just kept quiet, following Neeka's lead.

'All right,' Coach said. 'See you tomorrow.'

A few drops of rain started to pitter patter on our heads.

I inhaled the familiar smell of wet earth.

'Let's go,' Alexis said, gathering her water bottle and the extra T-shirt she'd brought. The rest of the team had already scattered. We packed up and took off to the locker rooms. Since we hurried out of there so fast and I found Momma already waiting for me in the school parking lot, I didn't get a chance to ask Neeka what was up.

Neeka, who usually bristled at the slightest instruction from Coach, falling into line so quickly?

No way. Maybe she'd just been playing it cool, too.

Before I jumped in the car I jabbed Neeka in the arm, trying to get a read.

She just smiled. I smiled back.

But on the inside, my heart was flip-flopping in my chest.

58.
OBLIVIOUS TO
THE OBVIOUS

The next day at lunch, Neeka called an emergency meeting. I was already at the table with my lunch waiting for Neeka to grab Luce, who was sitting two tables away with her cousin, Rosalie. They ate lunch together every single day.

'Aww man,' Luce groaned loud enough for the world to hear when Neeka walked over and yanked her up by the arm. 'Rosalie was in the middle of telling a crazy story. I'ma miss the juicy parts.'

'You'll get the juicy parts at home,' Neeka said, jerking her over. 'You live with Rosalie!'

'But it won't be the same,' Luce whined as she plopped herself down. 'It'll be the watered-down version.'

Neeka rolled her eyes and then scanned our faces. 'So, what are we gonna do?'

She stood at the front of our table with her foot on a chair.

239

Alexis and I looked at each other.

I pulled an apple from my brown paper bag, took a bite, and crunched.

'About what?' Alexis asked, carefree as a bee. She opened her lunch sack and pulled out her chicken sandwich. When she opened the tinfoil wrapping, my nose filled up with the red-hot spice.

'Laina,' I said, calmly at the same exact time Neeka whisper-screamed, '*Laina!*'

She cocked her head at Alexis, adding. 'Are you oblivious to the obvious?'

'I understand why you're freaking out,' I said, in between bites of apple. 'I was too. Still am, kind of. But the meet is in four days. At this point, all we can do is listen to Coach.'

I'd had the night to talk things over with Aunt Rose.

At the end of the day, she'd convinced me that being worried was normal, but I couldn't let it take over my life.

Neeka needed an Aunt Rose.

Still, I was relieved to know I wasn't the only one who was worried.

'Wrong answer,' Neeka said.

Ms Berry, who was on lunch duty, walked by and followed Neeka with her eyes – from head to toe. 'Foot down, young lady!' she said sternly.

Neeka took her foot off the chair and rolled her eyes again.

Luce flashed her small white teeth at Ms Berry's back.

Alexis stopped chewing her chicken and then said,

very calm, cool, and collected, 'It seems we've got two options.' She wiped the side of her mouth with her napkin and crossed her legs. 'We can give Laina the cold shoulder and scare her off so she doesn't want to run with us. I'm calling that Plan A for Asinine. Or we can practise passing with her like we're supposed to do and be nice. I'm calling that Plan B for Be Nice or, better yet, Plan B for Better. I know Laina better than you guys do. She has a little 'tude like you-know-who over there.' She pointed to Neeka. 'But she's cool. I'm not trying to be asinine. I vote for Plan B.'

'What does cool have to do with it?' Neeka said.

Neeka never, ever, ever wanted to practise handoffs with anyone else.

Not even alternates.

Every time we did practise with someone new, she made them miserable.

I put my apple core down on the table and raised my shoulders to my ears. 'We just have to practise with her and hope that Coach keeps me on the relay.' I deep sighed. 'I guess that means I'm voting for Plan Better or whatever Alexis just called it.'

'One shot left.' Neeka said. 'One!' She held up her pointer finger, looking around at each of us, then sat down, exasperated. 'We need to get her off.'

'That's not right!' Luce grumbled. 'It's wrong.'

'Correct, genius. That's the point. She's wrong.'

Luce frowned. 'Mamí taught me to not be a rough-neck because it makes no sense.'

241

'Does losing make sense?' Neeka argued back. 'Especially when we'll never run together again ever.' I took a deep breath when I heard Neeka's words. Even though I thought Alexis was right and I was voting for Plan Better, I couldn't forget about the one thing – win or lose – that wouldn't change: Luce was leaving.

'Come on, guys.' Alexis folded up her napkin like she always did. She looked at Luce. 'What's your vote?' Then she looked at Neeka. 'Yours, too?'

'Plan Better,' squeaked Luce, and then she held her fingers up like a cross in front of her face to protect herself from Neeka's scorching look.

Neeka gave Luce the stink eye. 'If we don't take control of this situation, it's gonna control us.' And she left it at that, slumping back into her orange seat and gesturing defeat.

I understood how Neeka felt better than anyone.

But I'd already learned the hard way and was learning still.

There were limits to what you could control outside of yourself.

Like Aunt Rose said, it was better to focus on working on your inside.

Right now, that meant learning to accept that Laina was a part of our team.

Whether we liked it or not.

59.
OUR NEWEST TEAM MEMBER

A few hours later, we were on the track, getting ready to practise drills with Laina, our newest team member. Coach told the five of us to wait at the back corner while he finished up a few things.

We walked over in silence.

When we got to the starting line, Neeka's jaw was clenched. She marched over to the fence and sat down alone, leaning her back against the metal.

I watched her take a sip of water from her water bottle and close her eyes.

Alexis stood next to Laina, and they decided to stretch some more.

Luce and I sat down on the track right where we were.

I pulled my legs up and wedged my chin between my knees. I whispered to Luce, 'Are we just not gonna talk?'

She looked around and shrugged.

After a few awkward minutes, Alexis walked up and crouched down between us.

She put one arm around Luce's shoulder and one around mine. 'Can't we just get started?'

'Coach said he'd be right back,' I said, waving my hands across her braids, which clickity-clacked.

Alexis breathed in and out slowly trying to gather patience like somebody's momma. 'He doesn't like when we wait around. Let's just go.'

Neeka must've had the same idea, because she walked over and nodded her head.

Luckily, Laina wasn't starting from zero.

She'd run the sprint medley relay before.

We started with an easy drill just to make sure we were all on the same page.

Neeka stood in for Coach and the four of us lined up single file.

She spaced us out within arm's reach, one right in front of the other.

We each stood with our feet together and moved our arms back and forth in a running motion. Alexis, who ran first, was at the back of the line holding the baton. When Neeka yelled, 'Go!' I moved my hand back to grab the baton from her. We all stayed right where we were, looking straight forward. We pumped our arms back and forth until Neeka yelled again, and I passed the baton to Laina. Then Laina passed to Luce, who was the last runner standing at the top of the line.

We kept on like that for a few times until Neeka stopped us.

'Laina,' she said, standing with her hand on her hips. 'You need to have your palm flat and wide open. And you're not holding the stick at the bottom like you should.' Laina's face wrinkled in confusion. 'And your arm's not going straight back. It's going off to the side. That's not how Coach Rosse taught us to pass.'

And your elbow has to be closer to your body . . .

And your hand has to be cocked . . .

And your thumb has to be down . . .

And your fingers have to be facing the outside . . .

I just stood there, watching everything in slow motion, hoping and praying no one exploded.

60.
GOOD HANDS

While my mind kept moving in slow motion, Neeka's words kept flying like fast-moving bullets.

A minute later, Laina turned to Neeka, her face dark. 'What's wrong with you? Why are you so hostile?'

Neeka was just about to answer when I snapped out of it and stepped in between the two of them. 'She's not trying to be, Laina. She's just telling you what Coach told us. Right, Neeka?'

I nodded briskly at Neeka. Her face was dialled to mad and stuck there.

Laina crossed her arms. 'Did he tell her to use that crazy voice?'

I took a breath. 'It wasn't crazy, Laina. She was just being . . .' I tried to think of the right word. Neeka's voice *had* sounded frustrated, but it wasn't totally crazy. Laina didn't understand that there was no mistaking Neeka when she got crazy. I didn't tell her that. Instead, I said, 'She was being passionate. Track is her passion.'

Laina crossed her arms. 'Well, she needs to *simmer down* with all that passion.'

Alexis flanked Neeka's other side. 'She's the fastest girl on the team so it's working for her. But maybe she could have said it a little better . . .'

Laina snapped her head. '*Better?*'

'Look, Laina,' I said. 'The truth is, if you want to run with us and be part of this relay team, you're gonna have to get used to it. This is how we do it. Warrior-style. Just like Coach always tells us. We all have our own roles on this relay team. And Neeka is kind of like the captain. That's how it's always been. And it's worked for us so far.'

Laina's eyes burned holes into my face just as Coach Rosse strolled up with his hands in his pockets.

He stopped in front of us. 'Glad to see you all didn't wait around. How's it going? Are we sticking those passes?'

Laina snorted. 'Well, actually,' she said, narrowing her eyes at Neeka and then at me and then waiting for what felt like forever. 'I guess I'm not doing it right. But the girls are trying to teach me.'

Coach took his hat off and put his arm on Neeka's shoulder. 'Well, with this one right here, you're in good hands.' He laughed. 'You girls got that, right? Hands . . . passing the baton . . .'

He chuckled some more.

We all rolled our eyes sky high.

Even Laina.

61.
DODGING BULLETS

'This whole season has been . . . ugh,' Neeka said back in the girls' locker room.

She was bending over on a bench, tugging at her laces.

I laughed. 'It'll be fine.' I sat down next to her and looked around to make sure no one else could hear us.

'Will it?' she said in a thin voice. 'And since when are you Ms Go-With-The-Flow?'

I thought about it.

Since I started listening to Aunt Rose?

Since I apologized to Neeka for throwing out the first dagger?

Since Odie and I finally made up?

Each of those things held their own note in my heart-song even though I still couldn't hear it all the way through.

I wasn't giving up though.

I was still . . . looking and listening for something.

I leaned my elbows on my knees. 'I don't know if I'm exactly going with the flow. But think about it. What can we actually do? Nothing. I'm just hoping I get to run with you guys. That's what really matters.'

Neeka squinted her eyes at me. She gripped the bench and looked down at her feet for a second. She exhaled. I could see the side of her face curving into a smile. 'Thank you for standing up for me, by the way. And maybe I was being a little hard on her. I'll say sorry tomorrow.'

We sat in silence for a minute.

'And, of course, you're gonna run,' Neeka said. 'Unless you break a limb, or a bird starts to nest in your hair because it thinks you're its home and your momma has to take you to a person who specializes in getting birds' homes off of people's heads.'

I shoved her with half my body. She shoved me back.

'I'm done fighting,' she said.

'Good. But we still want to fight to win, right?'

She grinned wider. 'Ms Go-with-the-Flow for two seconds.'

I smiled, putting my arm around her. 'Maybe we can try to win *and* go with the flow.'

Of course, I still wanted to win. I was just slowly starting to see that some things were more important. Like running together as a team.

That was being connected.

'OK. I'm down,' Neeka said a bit brighter. 'And I promise I'll be good with Laina. Now, back to your hair. I swear if we make it into the paper and you look like that, *you'll regreeeet it*.' She sang the last few words out so that the syllables multiplied.

Just then, Alexis and Luce appeared. Alexis sat on the bench across from us.

Luce squished in between Neeka and me, grinning. 'What's this I hear about the paper?'

'Wait,' Alexis said, putting her hand up like a stop sign and looking at Neeka and me in turns. 'You guys are talking about the paper again with that bullet we just dodged?' She shook her head. 'You guys are two crazy peas in a pod.'

'The other day,' I said, with a chuckle. 'I heard Aunt Rose say two peas in *the* pod.'

Luce looked at us quizzically. 'Wait . . . what's wrong with that?'

The three of us looked at each other and burst out laughing.

62.
KICKS

Neeka kept her promise. The very next morning, the four of us met up with Laina on the track before school started. We found her sitting at the starting line chugging a carton of chocolate milk.

'First,' Neeka said, looking down at Laina who was still guzzling. 'Sorry for getting so hot with you yesterday. Second, you sure you need all that milk? Doesn't seem like the best idea.'

Laina polished off the last of it, swiped her mouth and put the carton down. She stood. 'Thanks for saying sorry. And yeah, I always down a carton of milk before I run.'

We all looked at each other and shrugged. The apology seemed to go off without a hitch. And if drinking copious amounts of chocolate milk was as weird as Laina got, we'd be on easy street.

'OK, so how do you wanna start?' Neeka asked the group for the first time ever.

She usually just barked at us.

'I have an idea,' Laina said, raising her hand like she was in class. 'Why don't we do a practice run? Since Luce is leaving,' she looked at her with a sorry face, 'maybe she sits one out and I try to run her leg?'

Neeka nodded her head. 'Sounds smart to me.' She looked to Luce.

'You know that's fine with me,' Luce said.

Alexis and I looked at each other and nodded along.

'OK,' Neeka said. 'Let's warm up.'

We started walking.

'Oh,' Laina said. 'And I heard you guys had some sort of a special cheer at the last meet. Do I need to learn it?'

'Our chant,' I sighed. 'I don't think we're using that.'

'How do you know?' Luce piped up. 'I loved the chant. How about we vote on it.'

'Wait,' Neeka said, stopping and looking at Luce. 'Since when do you have permission to start asking people for votes? Isn't that my job?'

Laina looked a little worried.

'Don't worry,' I said to her motioning to lane one. 'We're not fighting. You'll know when we're fighting.'

Her face straightened out and she chuckled. 'OK. If you say so.'

When we got to practice that afternoon, Coach started us straight away.

The entire team warmed up.

We started and finished our drills.

It was only during the cool down that the commotion started.

I ran over to the fence to find Laina stooped over with her hand on her knees.

Neeka was yelling at her. 'Can you make it? Can you? Come on, man! Speak.'

I put my hand on Laina's back. 'What's . . . wrong? Make it . . . where?' I'd run so fast and was so out of breath each word had a long gap between it. I looked up at Neeka. 'Does she have asthma? Do we need to call Coach? An ambulance? What's going on?'

'She says she's feeling sick. I was trying to help her to the locker room but—'

'I guess you're not gonna make it,' Neeka said nonchalantly, as a stream of stringy liquid poured out of Laina's mouth all over my sneakers.

'Aw man,' I yelled, standing frozen.

I looked at my feet.

They were awash in chocolate milk and chocolate bits and chocolate pieces.

Luce sped over just in time. 'Not the kicks, man. Not the kicks.' She cupped her hands around her mouth, making it a bullhorn, and turned around. 'Alexis,' she yelled. 'Hurry up! Come see!'

I glared at Luce.

'It's OK,' Luce said looking back at me. 'I'ma help you out of those. But first I'ma laugh.' She turned to Laina. 'We warned you about chugging that chocolate milk, Kicks. But did you listen? *Nah!*'

Laina looked up with a strained face. 'Wait, who is Kicks?' Then, 'Oh no . . . it's happening again.' I stood there like a dummy, squeezing Laina's shoulder. More vomit rained down on my sneakers.

Alexis, who was squeamish and didn't like bodily fluids, kept her distance.

She shouted from very far away, 'Clean-up on lane six.'

'Good one,' Luce said, grinning wildly.

63.
A MESSY OPERATION

Aunt Rose was in the thick of cooking when I swung through the kitchen door after practice. 'I knew it was you,' she said as I walked to the table and sat down.

I squeezed my elbows in between casserole dishes and hand-mixers and baking trays. 'How?'

'I've studied how the family moves,' she answered, while kneading dough on the island countertop. 'Mama moves with air under her feet. Light touch. Baba moves fast on the way out, but slow and heavy on the return. And you, Kamaria, coming in or going out, you're like a monsoon.'

She laughed cheerfully while I did some studying of my own.

The kitchen was in the middle of a very messy operation. And I needed it.

Odie was coming over in an hour to help me with my school project for the Night of Learning. I hadn't told Aunt Rose anything about it because she'd inspired it and I wanted to surprise her with the finished piece at school tomorrow night.

But if I wanted to finish the project, I had to get her out of the kitchen.

Right now.

'How's schoolwork?' Aunt Rose said, giving me the perfect chance. She wiped her hands against her apron, and a cloud of flour rose up into the air.

'Funny you should mention school,' I said. She looked up at me for a second and smiled before returning her gaze to what she was kneading. I cleared my throat. 'I actually need to do my homework in the kitchen today.'

'I see,' she said with a knowing voice, even though she wasn't looking. 'So, you need to use the table?' She poured more flour into a bowl and let it sit. Next, she picked up a few cardamom pods and faced the stovetop. She plopped the pods into a skillet and turned the heat on medium.

'Yup. I do. And I kinda need privacy.'

She turned around and raised her eyebrows. 'Is it a secret?' She laughed. 'What about using that lovely desk in our bedroom?'

I picked up a metal attachment thingy that was near me and inspected it.

Other bits and bobs were spread out all over.

'It's not big enough for the project I'm working on,' I said, worried now that she wasn't taking the hint and couldn't read me. Which was weird because I thought we understood each other now. 'I need a big table with a lot of space to spread out. A *clean* space.' I waited a second. 'Odie's coming over, too.'

'Mmm hmm,' she said, spinning the skillet in circles over the flame. 'What project is this you and Odysseus are working on?'

'Just a science thing,' I answered cryptically.

Aunt Rose picked up the skillet and dumped the cardamom pods out onto the counter. Dough clung to her fingers. 'Perfect,' she said. 'You see here, Kamaria. You have to toast them . . . but not too much. You have to coax out the sweetness, like we sometimes have to coax the calves at home, *pole, pole*.'

She opened the pods one by one and poured the seeds into a small wooden bowl. She picked up a wooden stick that looked like a thick wand, and crushed the seeds, grinding and grinding them.

I shifted in my seat. 'By the time Odie gets here, we kinda need to—'

'Wait,' she cut in. 'I want to show you one thing. You see.' She tipped the bowl so that I could see inside. 'Now the seeds are a powder. As fine as dust.' She put the wooden bowl down and continued.

A small film of sweat was starting to bead around my neck when Aunt Rose looked up at me. 'Ten minutes. Everything will be clean.' Then, a few seconds later she said, 'And I will leave you and your very special friend alone without disturbing.'

She gave me a secret smile.

I blushed. 'Thanks.'

64.
A TWOFER

'You made some of the flamingos already, right?' Odie asked. It was an hour later, and we were sitting at a spotless kitchen table in front of my half-finished diorama.

'I tried one,' I said, shrugging sheepishly.

He sighed. 'Kamaria, there's no way –'

'Wait,' I stood up from the table and walked to the small, cluttered bookshelf in the corner where I'd stashed away all the other things we needed. 'Why are you calling me Kamaria again?'

It wasn't like I had to get used to being with Odie.

We had pretty much slipped back into our old ways.

Except for him calling me Kamaria.

'Aunt Rose calls you Kamaria,' he said, smirking.

'Aunt Rose and Baba. Not you.'

'But I like the sound of it.'

My stomach somersaulted, but I was quick on my feet. 'OK, *ODYS*-seus,' I said, emphasizing his name.

He nodded. 'I see your point.'

I sat back down in front of the materials and cracked my knuckles.

Time to get focused.

A month ago, I never thought I'd be doing a science project on Tanzania because what did I know about it except for school uniforms, all the freshest food on earth, and kids who actually respected their elders?

It was only after the way Aunt Rose waxed poetic about the 'immaculate night sky' of the Ngorongoro Crater, that I decided to switch my project.

The Grand Canyon couldn't compete.

And I wanted to thank Aunt Rose.

She had really helped me.

And she did it all while teaching-but-not-*teaching* me about Tanzania.

The Ngorongoro Crater was a huge, ancient volcano that had collapsed in on itself.

But as much as I had loved hearing about the night sky, replicating how the crater looked during the day made much more sense.

Especially since it was teeming with wildlife.

The best part was that I didn't have to spend too much time in the library.

I just asked Aunt Rose a ton more questions on the sly.

She ate it up.

She could go on and on about visiting the salty crater lake that had thousands and thousands of pink flamingos during the day and millions and millions of stars at night.

She told me about the savannah grasslands.

And the waterholes.

And seeing lions and rhinos and leopards for the very first time.

She talked about it like she'd been there yesterday.

Momma almost lost it when I told her what I'd been cooking up. 'Look at how much you've grown to connect to your home country,' she'd said. 'And it's only been a few weeks!'

I shook my head and rolled my eyes as she grabbed me in a tight hug.

Then she made an excellent point.

She said my diorama might be the only one about the entire African continent.

I would stand out.

Like the time I was the only girl in our grade to have fluorescent high-tops.

Momma knew I loved being original.

That was the icing on the cake!

I came up with a snazzy title for my project, Ngorongoro Crater: Salty Lakes, Pink-y Birds, and Wildly Wild Wildlife.

It was drawn in big chunky letters on the accompanying travel poster.

The main part of the project, the diorama, was mostly done, too.

Inside one shoebox, which was turned on its side facing front, I'd shredded pieces of twine to make dried grass for the crater floor. I also used my questionable art skills to make lions, elephants, zebras and rhinos out of

260

cardboard. The inside walls of the box were painted blue for the sky, with a few white puffy clouds. The shoebox sat inside of the shoebox lid, which was lying flat in front of us. This was where the salty lake and pink flamingos were going to go, spilling out from the crater.

The lake and birds were front and centre.

And since Odie was much better at arts and crafts than me, I had him on deck.

Everything we needed to use to finish up was on the table in front of us: black pipe cleaners, pink tissue paper, a glue stick, black and white markers, and pink card.

'So, where's the one flamingo you tried to make?' Odie asked, reaching over the tissue paper and grabbing some pink card. He drew the body of a flamingo with a sharp-ened pencil as easily as I breathed. It came out perfect.

'In the trash obviously. Why would I keep it when I have Michelangelo right here?'

He looked at me grinning. 'Oh, I don't know. Because it's your project.'

'Technically, we're allowed to work in pairs so . . .'

'Yup, and I guess we've always been a pair.' Odie looked down awkwardly.

My fingers fumbled over the markers while I tried not to make eye contact.

'You know . . . for this kind of stuff,' he said quieter.

I swallowed hard. And since Odie's eyes were turned downward, I let mine sweep over him for a second. His hair had grown longer. It was past his collar, which was popped. And I just noticed he was wearing a polo shirt.

Since when did Odie wear polos?

My stomach flopped again.

'Besides,' Odie said, breaking the silence and snapping me out of my thoughts. 'If we left this part up to you it would be a train crash.' He cracked a smile, and I wasn't sure if it was because he caught me watching him or because he was making fun of me.

I threw a marker at him across the table.

He didn't flinch. 'Cut,' he ordered instead, handing me the pile of card. He had already drawn five flamingos. 'So now, what are you, like an expert on Tanzania?'

I picked up the scissors and started cutting out the flamingos' bodies, one by one. 'Maybe. I feel like I never really knew anything about it before.'

Odie stopped drawing for a minute. 'But your dad's always talking to us about it.'

'You mean those long-winded lectures?'

Odie chuckled, starting up again. 'I guess.'

'Yeah, I think I blocked them out. Aunt Rose has a much better way with stories. Baba speaks in black and white and a ton of grey. He's so boring. Aunt Rose is all colour. She has a dreamy way of talking. And way more rhythm.' Odie nodded. And since he seemed really interested in what I was saying and I needed him to draw about fifty million more flamingos, and I wanted to avoid any more awkward silences, I kept going. 'I mean literally. Her words glide. I'm usually asleep half-way in. She needs two or three nights to finish one story.'

Odie picked up one of the flamingos I'd cut out and

shook his head. 'It's almost like you try to do it bad on purpose. I'm not cutting, too.'

'You mind your business and I'll mind mine.'

'Kamaria –'

I shot him a look.

'All right, all right. Kam,' he continued. 'Do I have to remind you again that all of this.' He pointed around the table. 'Is your business? Anyway, tell me more. Baba still owes me that trip to Tanzania for losing the bet about the Bulls last season. I know it's your country, but I don't want you knowing too much more than me.'

'OK. Well, I can say all my greetings.'

Odie looked at me, shocked. '*Really?*'

'Don't sleep.' I cut my eyes at him, but with a smirk on my face.

'OK, hit me.'

I sat up in my seat like Alexis and smiled. 'So, when you're greeting an elder, to show respect you say, *Shikamoo*.'

He nodded his hair back and then tossed some of the nuts Aunt Rose had left on the table into his mouth. He wiped the salt on his pants, which was so annoyingly Odie-like it made me smile. 'A twofer?' he said. 'You're learning the language *and* finally learning how to give due respect? What a deal.'

I threw Odie my 'you better watch it' face and he threw back a ball of crumpled pink tissue paper and only then did I realize how much better I felt about everything: Odie. Neeka. Aunt Rose. Running.

I felt lighter than I had in weeks.

Maybe months.

Which was a good thing.

Because I still had a lot on my plate.

65.
A NIGHT
OF LEARNING

It felt like a year had gone by since the regional meet, not a week and a half. But the end of track season wasn't the only thing we had to get through.

We had to finish the end of the school year, too.

Final exams, but before that, we had the Night of Learning.

The Night of Learning was my favourite school event, besides track meets.

Not because of the school projects, but because of the school spirit.

It felt different to be on our campus at night.

Special.

Momma, Aunt Rose and I made our way through the school's arched entrance at exactly five p.m., just as everything was getting started. I couldn't miss a minute. Not even to wait for Big Case Baba, who was coming late from work.

Aunt Rose couldn't get over how nice everything was.

The campus was glowing.

String lights looped from tree to tree and bobbed in the breeze.

A huge navy blue banner that read *The River Park Night of Learning* hung on the front of the main building. The school choir really made the night feel special, though. To welcome parents, they were giving a musical performance of the poem 'Afternoon on a Hill' on the quad's front lawn.

They blew everyone away with their voices.

They really looked the part too, in crisp white shirts with bow ties, black blazers and black pants.

'You'd have to be the President's children, or the President himself to attend such a function back home,' Aunt Rose told Momma as we strolled past them.

I guess it did feel like one big fancy garden party.

And it marked that point in the year – the almost end – when we could finally breathe. The teachers were more relaxed, too.

Some even smiled, making them seem human for a change.

Out of the corner of my eye, I caught Coach Rosse saunter by.

The fact that Coach showed up without his hat was a sure sign that he was off duty. His lips weren't pulled tight, either. He stopped walking as soon as he reached a small group of parents on the far side of the quad. I eyed them having a cheerful conversation. They must've been parents of students in his English class.

I was just about ready to go find Alexis when Coach Rosse started walking in our direction. 'Hello, Kam.' He squeezed my shoulder, and I smiled. Then he turned to face Momma. 'And Mrs. Kessy, so nice to see you.' He looked at Aunt Rose. 'I know we met very briefly at the track meet. It's nice to see you again . . . when I'm not under the starting gun.' He looked back to me and winked. 'You see what I did there Kam? Under the gun . . . or the starting gun . . . like race day.'

I couldn't roll my eyes at an adult in front of Momma, but I really wanted to.

I smiled.

Momma smiled, too. 'Yes, of course. This is Kam's aunt from Tanzania, Rose Kessy.'

Aunt Rose stuck out her hand.

Coach Rosse gave his signature handshake.

I thought Aunt Rose's arm would fall off.

His eyes lit up. 'I've always wanted to climb Mount Kili.' He leaned in closer to Momma and Aunt Rose and lowered his voice like he was telling them a secret. 'I hear it's a killer though!'

Then he laughed his corny joke laugh louder than I'd heard in a long time.

Aunt Rose smiled brightly. '*Karibu*. I hope you make it one day. In the meantime, Kamaria can tell you many things.'

'You heard that, Kam,' Coach Rosse said, widening his eyes and elbowing me. 'I'm ready to be taught! Well, it was lovely to see you all. I hope you enjoy what the students have done. And I look forward to seeing you at Saturday's meet.'

Before we knew it, he was dashing off to talk to another family.

'How friendly,' Aunt Rose said. 'He's like a Tanzanian.'

I shook my head and smiled, but I was starting to get antsy now.

Enough people had started to fill the quad that it was crackling like a fire.

The sound filled my ears.

That was my cue.

I waved goodbye to Momma and Aunt Rose and raced into the main building.

66.
THE GREATEST GIFT

I'd set up my diorama and travel poster hours ago and way before most of the other kids so I wouldn't have to do it after track practice. When I approached the hallway outside of our science class, I finally saw Odie's creation.

He'd chosen the rainforests of Borneo.

Only, he'd gone all out.

He'd stacked four shoe boxes on top of each other.

Each one a different layer of the rain forest.

Trees and miniature animals were made of cardboard and coloured card, down to the very last detail. Vines made of green yarn hung from one canopy to the next.

He used some real leaves and moss too.

Everything was labelled just so in his perfect handwriting.

The best part was the river.

It was simple. Just a million shiny, smooth, flat glass marbles coloured blue and some shimmery sea glass.

It was probably the best diorama in our science class.

Maybe even in the whole grade.

I was just about to peek my head inside my old science teacher's classroom when I felt a tap on my back.

I turned around to find Baba standing there grinning from ear to ear. 'Momma says we're in for a treat, Kamaria.'

Aunt Rose and Momma stood behind him.

'I don't know about that,' I said, trying to fight a smile.

Aunt Rose scooted around Baba. 'I'm sure it will be magnificent since it was such a big secret. Only Odysseus could see.' She smiled. 'Now show us! Which one is yours?'

I debated whether I should start with Odie's and then ease my way down the line.

His was right in front of us, but I decided it was too impressive.

Mine might be a let-down afterwards.

While we shuffled down the hallway, I explained the theme of the night again and before I knew it, we were standing in front of my table.

I heard a loud gasp.

Aunt Rose's hands were covering her mouth.

She dropped them, still in shock. 'Ngorongoro! You made Ngorongoro!'

I bit back a smile and nodded.

I turned around to find Momma and Baba holding hands, grinning.

Aunt Rose gave me a hug and then pulled back with a serious look on her face. 'We who are called to tell stories usually hope our audience is also called to listen. And sometimes, we pray for something bigger. That they can listen wholly with their heart. That is, we hope they can feel what we say, connect to it, not just hear it. It is the greatest gift. It is what you have given me today.'

When Aunt Rose let me go, her eyes looked misty.

I didn't know what to say.

I was about to take her hand when Odie poked his head over Momma's shoulder. 'Don't let her take all the credit. A couple of those pink flamingos were mine. The good-looking ones.'

Everyone laughed and I was glad for the distraction.

I'd never seen Aunt Rose this emotional.

'OK, folks,' Odie continued. 'When you're done *oohing* and *aahing* and being totally blown away by Kam's amazing project, I have something else to wow you.'

'You seem very confident,' I said, putting my hands on my hips.

'I am,' Odie whispered so only I could hear him. He leaned in closer. 'Have you seen my rainforest?'

I shook my head. 'You're the worst.'

Odie threw his arm over my shoulder and looked at me cockeyed. '*Really?*'

My heart started pounding so hard in my ears I almost didn't hear Baba chiming in. 'Odysseus is right, Kamaria. This is something else. A beautiful rendering. I guess it's safe to say that Aunt Rose has done a spectacular job of showing you home. Better than I have.'

I shrugged. 'Aunt Rose and I speak the same language.'

271

Aunt Rose winked at me.

Baba nodded. 'It seems so. Now please tell us all about it. I haven't been to Ngorongoro in many, many years. I think you have already convinced me to make it a priority!' I scooted around to the travel poster and got ready to run through everything I'd learned that made the Ngorongoro Crater a world-class travel destination.

Other kids started to gather round and even a teacher or two.

But instead of being frozen stiff like I normally would be in front of an audience, I stood a little taller and kept my eyes glued on the front row.

Momma and Baba and Aunt Rose and Odie.

67.
IF YOU HAD A CRYSTAL BALL

Afterwards, I took Momma and Baba and Aunt Rose around to all the good projects and eventually the learning part of the night came to a close.

I went to find the girls straightaway.

Alexis and Luce were outside of the sixth-grade science class talking to Mr Josephs-Ivory. All four of us had him for science last year, and although he was one of my favourite teachers of all time, I didn't stop to chat. I smiled a hello and quickly pulled the girls away by their sleeves so we could find Neeka. We had to search high and low but finally found her in the gym shooting free throws with a few eighth graders.

The screech of squeaky shoes on the wooden floor echoed loudly.

We sat down in the first row of bleachers and watched.

Somebody zipped the ball to Neeka. She squared up her shoulders and shot.

The tips of her feet floated in the air for a second as the ball sailed up high and curved like a rainbow. Neeka had seen us walk in, so as soon as the ball swished through the net, she gave the other girls high-fives and ran over.

We made it outside to the quad just in time to catch the sun's final hoorah.

Sherbet orange and rose melted across the sky.

After we plopped ourselves down on the glossy green grass, I spread my legs out wide. The pleats of my skirt fell in-between my legs.

Neeka and I were the only ones wearing skirts and sneakers.

Neeka had on pom-pom socks for a little extra cuteness.

Alexis and Luce stuck with the unofficial dress code and wore regular dresses like most of the other girls.

We didn't talk about Coach Rosse's bad jokes.

Or the state championship two days away.

We didn't talk about fighting or losing or winning.

We mostly talked about how fast the year was ending.

We could count the weeks left on one hand.

Then we'd officially be rising eighth graders.

Next year would be our last year before high school.

For Luce, the change would be even more dramatic.

'Can you believe it?' I said, flipping my pleats back and forth in my lap.

Flipping and flipping and flipping and flipping.

The rhythm felt good in my hands.

'I'm ready for high school,' Luce said. 'I wish I could

blink and fast forward past eighth grade. At least I'll still have my cousins with me next year.' She looked at us with puppy dog eyes. I gave puppy dog eyes back.

'So,' Neeka said. She sat up a little straighter. 'If you had a crystal ball and could see into the future, what one thing would you want to know? Alexis, you go first.'

Alexis shrugged her shoulders. 'Nothing really. I'm not dying to know what's gonna happen when I grow up. Dessa's life doesn't look so great. If that's where I'm headed, I don't want to know about it. But I guess I'd wanna know when I'll have a boyfriend. And what he'll look like. And if he'll be Bajan. Because I don't know any Bajan boys that are cute.'

Neeka looked at her hands and grinned to herself, like Alexis had given her something scintillating to chew on. Then she said, 'That's more than one thing, but OK. Luce, you're next.'

Luce scrunched her nose. '*Hmm*. I know you guys think I'd ask something obvious. Like will I like my new life once we move? Or will I like school? Or will I still be the best jumper in the universe ever?' Luce shimmied her shoulders, and we laughed. 'But, nope. I'd want to know something real practical. Like how tall I'm gonna end up. Like, am I gonna be this short forever? I'm *so* tired of being puny.' We laughed again, louder this time.

'Better too small than too tall,' I said.

Neeka looked in my direction. 'All right, Kam, you?'

When I looked at the girls, I felt my heart thumping. The one thing I wanted to know about the future was a no-brainer. It's why I'd been so set on winning. It's what I was afraid of all along. I took a deep breath. 'I guess I just want to know if we'll always be friends. Especially you, Luce, since you're the one who's boating away.'

Alexis scooted closer to me and put her arm around my shoulder. 'You know we'll always have each other's back.'

'Better believe it!' Luce chimed in, which made me grin but want to cry at the same time.

Neeka snorted a laugh.

Alexis looked at her. 'Your turn.'

Neeka pulled out a thick blade of grass and ran it between her fingers. She shook her head. 'Nothing.'

Alexis made a face. 'You are not for real. *Nothing?* You don't want to know *anything* about the future.'

'Nah,' Neeka said. She tore the blade of grass in half. 'It's gonna come anyway. I'll just wait and see.'

'OK Ms Profound,' Alexis said. 'While you're *waiting* and *seeing* for your bright future, can you help?' She shook the ends of her braids.

Alexis's beads had to come off before the meet.

It was an official rule.

Beads weren't allowed during races.

Not if they dangled like the way Alexis wore them.

Alexis backed right up into Neeka's lap.

Luce and I crowded around her, pulling off tiny black elastics and wooden beads and dropping them into an empty plastic shopping bag and chatting about randomness.

A few minutes later, Laina rolled up, smiling. 'Can I help?'

I moved over and made space.

'Appreciate the help, Kicks,' Alexis said. 'Just don't vomit in my hair.'

The four of us smirked.

Laina laughed her little laugh. 'Uh yeah. I'm really sorry again, Kam.'

'Don't worry about it,' I said. 'I got a new pair of sneakers out of it. I should probably thank you. Besides, did we ever tell you about how Neeka got her first nickname, Purple Rain?'

'Oh, no you didn't,' said Neeka, swirling her head at me in an exaggerated way.

'Oh, yes she did,' said Luce swirling back even crazier.

Neeka went to kick Luce, but before she got to her, Luce took off running.

'I never knew all of y'all acted so crazy,' Laina said, laughing.

Alexis turned around with her half-beaded head. 'You don't know the half.'

68.
A FLASH DECISION

By the time we were done with Alexis's hair, food was being served. Momma, Baba and Aunt Rose had already found their way to a patch of grass and were chatting away with Aunt Darien. Baba kept bringing them little plates piled high with snacks. I saw Aunt Rose licking a snowy crust of sugar from a cookie and then taking a small bite. She smiled to herself afterwards. Momma kept her left hand at the bottom of Baba's neck and nibbled with her right. This was usually how she ate when she socialized.

Luce poked me and whispered, 'Look.' She nodded her head in their direction. 'Your parents are so cute.' We were sitting on the grass in the opposite corner.

I rolled my eyes and smiled.

I was used to them. What I was not used to was how relaxed Baba seemed.

Either the magic I felt in the air was super contagious or something else was going on. Baba would never tell, but my guess was he had a break in his big case. I was even more sure of it on the car ride home when he and Momma made a flash decision to go out.

They hadn't done that since Baba started burning the midnight oil.

'We'll have our fun while they have theirs,' Aunt Rose said after they dropped us off at home. She waved to them from the stoop with one hand and clutched a white paper bag filled with more desserts in the other while they drove off into the warm night.

69.
SPELLBOUND

The house was quiet and dark as we slipped off our shoes and snaked our way through to the kitchen. Aunt Rose flipped on the light switch and made a beeline for the stove.

It was like her homing device.

I sat down by the open window and drew the curtain back. I didn't see stars, but the moon was shining brightly, like a beacon.

I turned my attention back to Aunt Rose who was engrossed in one of her favourite rituals: making chai, which was spiced tea.

She pulled a saucepan from the bottom cupboard and filled it with water.

Then she placed it on the burner.

The smell of gas came up and quickly faded.

After rummaging through the fridge and a million plastic bags on the counter, Aunt Rose quickly threw her finds in the water. With all the cups of tea she drank, I could identify everything blindfolded now: a few small rounds of fresh ginger, two cinnamon sticks, a few cloves, and some cardamom pods.

Aunt Rose turned to me. 'Cup?' I usually didn't drink tea, which she knew.

But tonight, I nodded.

She walked over to the island and pulled over a metal tin from the bread box filled with mandazi, fresh as anything. They reminded me of the very first batch she made on her second night here.

Back when I was going berserk trying to come up with the chant.

Before we lost hard at the regional meet.

She came over and placed the tin in the centre of the kitchen table.

I relaxed deeper into my chair and watched as she walked back to the stove.

Tea bags went into the pot and then, a few minutes later, milk.

Sugar was the last magic touch.

The sounds of voices from the street below floated up and through the window.

They scratched in my ear.

All this time, Aunt Rose and I barely talked.

When I moved through my race-night ritual I preferred quiet too.

Finally, when everything was done, Aunt Rose pulled two cups from the cupboard and poured the spicy tea.

She dropped a spoon in each cup and brought them back to the table.

I was just about to take a sip when Aunt Rose said, 'Blow, *kipenzi*,' with her honey-sweet voice. I smiled.

She sometimes had a way of talking to me like I was a baby.

But she never made me feel like one.

Instead, I felt cared for.

Special.

Beloved, like she called me.

Kipenzi.

'When we were young,' Aunt Rose started, 'Baba was always the planner with a dream. His big dream was to study in America. But you, like I've told you before, are a dreamer with a plan.' She stirred the milky hot liquid, crinkling her brows as she blew.

I opened my mouth to say something, then closed it.

Aunt Rose waited.

I put my cup down and rested my hands on the table. 'It can't always be about me Aunt Rose. What about you? Is there anything you want to talk about?'

Aunt Rose was so emotional when she saw my project.

I was sure something was up.

Maybe she missed Tanzania.

Maybe she missed her kids.

Maybe she missed her rolling stone of a husband.

Aunt Rose smiled. 'Not tonight, Kamaria. But thank you for asking.'

'OK,' I sighed, wondering if she was really OK.

I went to switch the light off so we could see more of the moonlight then relaxed back into my chair, deciding to trust the part of me that said I should just give her space.

If someone had told me weeks ago that I'd be in the kitchen, spellbound by an aunt I'd just met making something as simple as tea, I'd say they were nuts.

But in a small way, it already felt like I'd known Aunt Rose forever.

It was in the way she spoke to me, like she could see right through me.

Straight to the best and worst parts.

Maybe that's why it was easy to sit in silence with her.

Both of us in our own worlds while night pooled around us.

Usually, all the things that were up in the air and that I wanted to know would be a swarm.

Questions about the state meet . . . finding my true rhythm . . . our team without Luce . . . the twitchy feeling I had every time I saw Odie . . . Aunt Rose and Tanzania already feeling like home.

But tonight, they weren't shaking me up as much.

I looked across the table and figured I had Aunt Rose to thank for a lot of that.

Then I thought of something else.

Maybe Aunt Rose was in her own swarm sometimes, too.

Like that time she seemed filled with sorrow and tonight when she saw my project.

Maybe even right now.

But maybe she'd found the stillness like she'd taught me to do.

And then something else hit me.
Being still in the swarm.
Now that was a completely different rhythm altogether.

70.
KIPEPEO

'*Njoo*,' Aunt Rose said on Friday morning before school. She patted the space beside her.

'OK,' I said, tumbling out of bed. Butter yellow sunlight fell through the windowpane, spreading across the carpet and onto my feet.

I was sitting so close to her only a thread of air could pass between us.

The bedspread was so crisp, I almost didn't want to move and wrinkle it.

Aunt Rose put her hand on my leg, and I could feel her warmth beside me. 'In my home, we have a rule. We pray before something important. The first time you raced, I was new to you. But now you know me.'

The Kessys and their rules.

Baba had the same one – only he was the one who prayed, not me and Momma.

I'd never prayed in a real sense. 'Dear God' kind of praying.

But I talked to the Universe and Mother Earth all the time.

Which seemed like the same thing.

'OK,' I said, without thinking too much about it.

Aunt Rose took my hand into hers. 'Close your eyes and I'll start.'

After Aunt Rose finished, she brought me another kanga.

'Did you pack a whole suitcase of them?' I asked as she sat back next to me and flung the kanga open over our laps. I never knew when she'd give me another one but I looked forward to it. It had become one of our rituals.

'I packed many. I still have some of my mother's, you know. But these were all chosen specifically for you. Even though I didn't know the whole of you when I bought them.'

I studied the colours and the words on the kanga.

It was bright yellow with a red mandala pattern around the border.

There was a red rectangle in the middle and inside of it, a diamond and dot motif. At the bottom of the rectangle, the saying read:

Kila kipepeo huruka na mbawa zake.

The only word I knew was *kipepeo.*

Butterfly.

I touched the word with my finger and glanced over at Aunt Rose. 'What does the saying mean?'

She put her hand on my leg. It felt heavy. 'There is always more than one way to think about these things,' she said. 'The literal translation is, "Every butterfly flies with its own wings". It may also mean that each person has their own unique way of doing things. And I think it has another meaning: we can each depend on ourselves to soar.'

I nodded, letting it sink in.

Aunt Rose added quickly, 'And by soar, I don't mean win. If you are flying your own path in your own direction and you lose, you are still soaring.'

Later that night, I looked down at the flapjack Momma dumped on my plate and cut it into small pieces. I was already full, but started forking more food into my mouth, anyway.

'So,' I told Aunt Rose between bites, explaining how the state meet would work. 'Lots of waiting just like the last one. The girls and I will each run our own races, except for Luce who jumps, and then the relay will be at the end.'

Aunt Rose clapped. 'I can't wait to see you run again. I used to play netball in primary school, you know.'

I looked at her suspiciously. '*You did?* You never told me that.'

She nodded. 'Don't look so surprised!'

I laughed. 'I'm not . . . OK, I am.'

'Kamaria,' Aunt Rose said, every square inch of her face lighting up. 'You're not the only talent in the house.' Momma and Baba laughed now too. 'Now what should I wear for good luck?'

'Oh, anything you want,' I said. 'If you have anything in our school colours, orange and black, that would be great.'

Aunt Rose considered this while folding her napkin. A satisfied grin spread over her face. 'Orange is not my friend. But I think I have something that will work.'

Everyone was quiet for a moment before Baba started speaking. 'I know I've been busy with work, Kamaria.' He drummed a beat with his fingers on the dining table. 'But I'm looking forward to tomorrow.'

'OK,' I said, swiping my finger around the edge of my plate to get the last bits of maple syrup. I put my finger in my mouth and licked it off.

Baba continued. 'And I'm proud of all that you've done this year. With school, track and everything else.' He smiled at me as he picked up his glass. He took a sip of water before he continued. 'And I'm especially glad that you've shown Aunt Rose such a good time. She's told us that you have been the highlight of her visit so far.' He tapped the table with his glass when he put it back down.

The ice rattled.

'It's true, Kamaria,' Aunt Rose said. 'You've been the balm I needed. You are the heartbeat of this home.' She smiled. 'Well . . . not just here. I'm sure your friends would agree. You are the force that keeps them connected . . . and on track . . . too.'

I blushed.

And then I thought, Is Aunt Rose making corny track jokes like Coach?

71.
RACE NIGHT

Tonight, my race-night ritual was pretty much the same as it always was. I might have been living a little more on the fly, but my routine was still important, and I ticked everything off in my head before heading upstairs.

Flapjacks and biscuits? Check.

Ten red jellybeans from Baba's study? Check.

Running shoes laced up and sitting by the front door, facing the street? Check.

Even Odie called to give me a hard time, in a good way.

And when my heart sped up at the sound of his voice, it didn't drive me nuts.

It felt almost . . . normal.

A different kind of normal.

In bed, after I climbed between the sheets and wrapped the *kipepeo* kanga Aunt Rose gave me over my pillow-case, tomorrow's race didn't replay in my mind over and over again like it usually would.

No needling thoughts.

No swell of panic looming over me.

Instead, random thoughts floated through my head like fast-passing clouds until I started to get drowsy.

That's when I saw it.

A perfect butterfly.

It was flitting behind my eyelids in the same colours as the *kipepeo* kanga.

Red and yellow.

Then the butterfly was me and I was the butterfly.

I felt myself lifting off.

I was soaring higher and higher and higher until I decided it was time to come back home. But I couldn't land.

Instead, I vanished into a whirl of orange.

The image only lasted for a second before it disappeared.

My eyes blinked open one last time.

I curled my knees up into my chest.

Eventually the wheels in my head ground to a complete stop.

The tiredness had seeped so deep into my bones that I didn't hear Momma, Baba and Aunt Rose turning off the TV and climbing up the stairs.

I didn't even hear the doorknob click when Aunt Rose came into our room.

I was already fast asleep.

72.
ROCKY START

Early Saturday I woke up in a fit. I was worried that the sky might have fallen to pieces overnight, and everything would be over before it started.

But when I looked out the window, there was the cotton-candy sky.

Swirls of pink and blue.

Perfectly in place.

After a few steadying breaths in the car ride over to school, I was ready for the state championship. I was hoping Alexis, Neeka and Luce were ready too. But when Momma and I drove up to the school parking lot, I found the three of them sitting on the kerb looking anything but.

Yes, they were dressed in their singlets and shorts.

But they were also holding their windbreakers over their heads for shade.

About to get heatstroke.

Before I could jump out of the car to save them,

Momma leaned over to give me a kiss. 'It's already steaming. Did you bring sunscreen?'

'*Momma*,' I said, tugging on the door handle. It was always stuck when I needed to make a run for it. 'You know I stopped wearing sunscreen.'

She looked over at me. 'Yes, and I know you're still half of me and I burn. Borrow some . . . and good luck, although you don't need it!'

She smiled as I opened the door and jumped out of the car with my backpack. Then she rolled down her window and stuck her head out. 'See you girls later!'

The horn honked twice as she drove off.

'Why aren't you guys sitting in the shade?' I asked, as I came up to the sidewalk, huffing. I had to squint against the sun. I stood right over Alexis. At least she was sipping on some water.

Neeka glared up at me from under her windbreaker. 'We were. Coach just told all of us two minutes ago to come over here . . . The bus is late. Besides, aren't you the one cutting it close?'

I rolled my eyes.

Neeka knew I only lived a few blocks away, and I always had perfect timing.

But she was right about one thing.

The school bus should've been here by now, waiting.

The bus driver *was* late.

Steamy morning.

Late bus.

This felt like a rocky start.

292

Neeka stood up. 'Gotta pee. Be right back.' I watched her jog off and disappear behind the double doors.

Five minutes later, I heard a heavy engine rumbling, followed by squealing brakes. I picked up Neeka's backpack from the sidewalk and yanked Alexis and Luce up before I even saw the yellow bus turn into the parking lot.

'Shouldn't we wait for Neeka?' Alexis asked, trying to keep up with me as I raced to the bus. Its doors folded open.

'She knows where to find us,' I said, turning my head. 'And we need to get our seats.'

We climbed on to the bus and walked all the way back to the last row where we always sat. I dropped into my seat like a wet rag and let my lungs deflate. Then I shoved my backpack and Neeka's under the seat in front of us. 'What kind of bus driver shows up late on the day of a state championship?' I muttered to myself.

Luce heard me. She and Alexis were sitting across from me. 'Maybe he had to stop for snacks,' she said innocently. 'Or maybe he had to use the pee-pee room like Neeka.' Of all the things I loved about Luce, I'd miss her way of saying things most.

The rest of the team piled in and filled up the seats.

Voices breezed across the aisle as everyone settled.

Laina waved to us before sitting down with her crew.

We had a long bus ride ahead of us.

I looked out of the window and saw Neeka flying towards the bus.

Coach waved her on with his clipboard.

She quickly ran up the steps.

He followed right behind her and did a quick mental count.

Everybody was here.

Coach signalled to the bus driver.

The doors hissed shut.

Neeka had to shuffle past some of the other girls to get to the back.

I watched her bonk Laina on the head with a water bottle before she plopped herself down next to me, her breath coming in quick bursts.

The familiar hint of her baby powder started to set my mind at ease.

After a second, she looked at me. 'Are you calm Kam or crazy Kam right now?'

I pulled her backpack up from the floor and gave it to her. 'Crazy-calm Kam.' I answered back. 'You?'

She smiled, opening the front pocket of her backpack and fishing out a ponytail holder. She bent her neck down and pulled her hair high on top of her head, wrapping one bobble around and over the other so it stayed fastened.

Her ponytail tumbled down to the bottom of her back.

'I'm ready,' she said finally. She relaxed back into the seat. 'Ready to win.'

73.
DO NOT LOOK

The air was even thicker by the time we filed off the bus. I felt a line of sweat snaking down my back as we dodged throngs of people.

Runners of all stripes were warming up.

Coaches and parents and spectators were everywhere.

We didn't waste time, though.

We cut right through the mobs and got straight to our first warm-up.

I can't lie. My feet stuttered those first few steps. As we looped around on the grass, my breath came out like staccato notes, all disconnected and disjointed. But eventually my chest and legs loosened, and I found my groove.

Then, just as we rounded the curve, we spotted her.

Neeka's archenemy.

Our fiercest competitor.

And the biggest threat to our blue ribbon.

Crazy-Cold Eyes.

She and her girls were sitting ahead of us on the edge of the grass with their school uniforms, matching racing shoes *and* matching hairstyles.

Neeka, who was jogging on my left, turned as stiff as a corpse.

As they came closer into view, I swallowed my words instead of saying out loud what I really thought. Which was, they were a sight to behold.

They were majestic flyness if I'd ever seen it.

From top to bottom.

All four girls had long box braids decorated in their school colours and beads.

We all knew we couldn't wear beads dangling from the ends of our braids.

They had been known to fall out and roll around the track.

Alexis groaned on Thursday night when I bit the final elastic off of her braid and caught the last of the beads as they slipped down into my palm.

But Crazy-Cold Eye's crew had cleverly used ribbons looped through a few bright yellow beads, which were then woven through their braids securely.

That meant they were accents and not accidents waiting to happen.

Just when we were about to pass alongside them, Neeka pinched my arm. 'Whatever you do, DO. NOT. LOOK,' she ordered all three of us through clenched teeth.

Alexis and Luce nodded.

But I couldn't help it.

Crazy-Cold Eyes sat with her legs folded to the side, her arms back, and her chin in the air. She squeezed her teammate's arm as we rolled by, and I could hear them snickering. With an unflinching gaze, Crazy-Cold Eyes lifted her right hand and made an L with her forefinger and thumb. I watched as she mouthed the word, 'Loser.'

A small ripple waved through my stomach.

I didn't dare tell Neeka.

If we lost, she'd say it was because I looked Crazy-Cold Eyes in the eyes when I knew better. Instead, I tried to stay calm and kept it moving.

But I wouldn't forget.

74.
CRASH LANDING

Like we did at all the track meets we'd ever competed in, we waited. And waited. And waited. And waited some more. That was the way it always went.

I tried to get in the zone and put my headphones on.

At one point, I was jolted out of my haze by Neeka, who was elbowing me. 'Wanna watch Alexis? She's about to be up.' I nodded yes, but the truth was I wanted to stay in my own head a little longer.

'Hurry up,' Neeka said, standing up and walking a few steps down for a closer view.

'Give me a minute,' I said, moving a little slowly.

When I heard the starting gun go off, I stood up faster and uncoiled my headphones from around my neck. I walked down to Neeka, who was jumping and yelling and cheering and practically about to fall over the metal railing.

I was just about to open my mouth when my eyes bugged out of my head.

It took a moment for me to register what was going on. It was happening so fast I almost missed it.

Alexis's right leg had just whipped up but then her back leg got tangled on the second-to-last hurdle. She was crumpled on the track now, holding her ankle. I could hear her shrieking. Coach and some other support staff were running over to her. A look of panic flashed across Neeka's face and froze there.

'What just happened?' I stuttered.

I couldn't move. I was still in shock.

Neeka had one hand covering her mouth and the other pointing in the direction of the track. 'Alexis!' she said.

75.
WHAT REALLY MATTERS

I looked around the chaotic bleachers for Luce. My head was zooming in all directions.

I couldn't think straight. I couldn't catch a steady beat.

Alexis had already been moved off the track and was somewhere getting fixed.

But what about Luce.

Was she still jumping?

I used my hands to shield my eyes against the sun.

There she was!

Luce was standing on the grass running her mouth and hamming it up.

I motioned to her with my hands like a wild woman.

After a few seconds, and by some miracle, she saw me through the million events that were happening all at once. She started walking over.

Faster, Luce!

I motioned faster.

Come on. Come on.

Luce started to run.

By the time she slipped past our other teammates, she was half-grinning, half-scowling, and out of breath. 'What's up?' She looked from me to Neeka.

Neeka's face was buried in her hands.

Luce frowned, huffing.

I started grabbing up my things and stuffing them into my backpack. 'Alexis fell during her race. A real crash landing. It looked like she hurt her ankle. We have to make sure she's OK.'

Luce started nodding, wide-eyed.

'She probably can't walk,' I said. 'Definitely can't run. We'll need to grab Laina, talk to Coach, and figure out what to do for the relay now, before Neeka and I run our race.' I was already pushing my way down the bleachers, leaving Luce and Neeka to get their stuff and catch up.

The five of us were back behind the bleachers by the East Entrance, huddled in a circle. Alexis was standing on one foot and leaning against Luce so she could avoid putting pressure on the other, which was taped around the ankle.

I was sweating bullets, trying to breathe. 'So, you're gonna be OK?'

Alexis swatted at me. 'You heard Coach. Me gwan be fine,' she said in a Bajan accent. 'A little sprain. Let's just focus on the relay before you and Neeka have to go.'

Thank goodness for Dum Dum Alexis always being calm in the clutch.

I knew she was screaming on the inside about her ankle.

Even though Coach did make it sound like she'd be OK.

He *had* also said that it made most sense for Laina to take the first leg. And then, with a wink, he said that he'd let us talk it over. He'd be willing to listen to us if we came up with a different plan, but there was no guarantee he'd go with it.

I took a deep breath and looked at Neeka and then Luce and then Laina. 'What's the plan? Laina, I think you have to take first leg like Coach said. It doesn't make sense for Luce to switch legs. Or me. And Neeka has to be anchor. I know running first isn't your strong suit, but . . .'

Laina nodded, looking nervous. 'Yeah, it's not . . . but I guess I can do it.'

I took a deep breath.

I had to find a way to keep this wheel on its track.

No.

Rhythms change. That's what Aunt Rose had said.

And every butterfly flies with its own wings.

I had to find a way to keep *myself* on track.

How?

I put my hands on Laina's shoulders and looked her in the eye. 'The worst thing that can happen is you botch the hand off. Lucky for you, I've already done that once, right?'

She kind of nodded.

'Right?' I asked again, firmer this time.

She smiled and laughed her little laugh. 'Yeah, I guess so.'

'Besides,' I said. 'I got over it, and once I did, I think it helped me to see that running together . . .' I looked over at Alexis's bad ankle and smiled nervously '. . . and being the best teammates to each other is what counts!'

'She's right,' Alexis said, half smiling and half grimacing. 'I've been saying that since the get-go.'

I smiled at her and focused my eyes on Neeka.

Her eyes weren't raging. Or dark.

They were smooth as glass.

Was that the calm before the storm, or the calm after the storm?

I couldn't tell.

'What do you think, Neek? We got this, right?'

She thought for a second. 'Only thing we have to do before our race is teach Laina the chant.'

I started shaking my head. 'No, no, no! We are not doing the chant.'

Luce stepped closer to me, while Alexis hopped over on one foot to Neeka. 'It's my last race with you. We're keeping the chant.'

I inhaled.

We didn't lose the regional meet because of the chant.

We wouldn't win the state meet because of it, either.

Our connection to running and to each other . . .

Our circle, on and off the track . . .

Our rhythm and flow . . .

My rhythm and flow . . .

This is what really mattered.

The chant could boost our team spirit though. That couldn't hurt. And since Alexis wasn't with us, it was a way for her to be on the track, too.

Laina and I looked at each other. She gave me two thumbs up. 'Teach it to me. I'm on drill squad. I can catch steps quick.'

'OK,' I said.

Neeka nodded to a quiet area. 'Let's go.'

76.
THE FREEDOM
OF FLYING

'Runners for the 4 x 100 relay . . .' a staticky speaker shouted out a few hours later.

This was our cue.

The bleachers were chock-full and the air all around us was magnetic.

Laina, Neeka, Luce and I jumped up from the warm metal bench.

Neeka had a little extra pep in her step because she came in first for the one-hundred-metre dash. And even though, I came in third place, I was just happy my legs crossed the finished line.

I turned to Alexis.

She was smiling from ear to ear. 'Make me proud, dummies! And Kam, way to be calm, cool and collected. You're my girl on the fly now!'

I shook my head, gave her a quick squeeze. The rest of

the girls squeezed around me and gave Alexis high-fives before we made our way down.

'We got this,' Neeka said as we stepped on to the grass.

Her voice was gruff and clipped in the way it was when she was completely focused. She kicked a paper cup out of her way like it had committed a crime and scanned the field.

'Over there,' she said, pointing to a small patch of free space.

We marched over to the spot and formed our usual circle.

Except this time, Laina was to my right instead of Alexis.

I stood frozen for a minute and took a few frightened breaths.

My jaw was clacking with fear.

My legs turned to Jell-o.

I ran my eyes over the bleachers and tried to sift through the crowd in the stands, but it was impossible in the sea of faces.

There was no way I could spot Momma, Baba, Aunt Rose and Odie.

I could barely see Alexis and I knew where she was sitting.

My mind shuffled for a minute.

I made a quick prayer for Alexis's ankle, then thought of Aunt Rose.

I hoped she was beaming her smile all the way over to me like she promised.

I closed my eyes, taking a sharp breath, and out of habit gripped the fingers in my right hand tightly.

Laina squeezed back.

I opened my eyes and gave her a thank you smile for returning the favour.

I exchanged looks with Luce.

I knew we hadn't even started the race, but it already felt like the end to me.

Three years of running together and everything in between.

Mostly laughing.

And that was mostly because Luce could find the bright side of anything.

Luce was the pitch-perfect note in our heartsong.

I could always hear her. And she could always hear me.

Before my mind dug deeper into its memory bank of us, they announced the start of the race.

Neeka looked up. 'We got this,' she said again. 'It's ours.'

We nodded.

A warm breeze whipped over our heads.

It was time for the chant.

We had practised it in the same exact way that we did at the regional meet: one round together, and then repeating rounds.

I took in another breath, and we started.

We got head deep – clap, clap, clap
We went heart deep – clap, clap, clap

We dug soul deep – clap, clap
To win this meet – clap, clap, clap

As we fanned out to our positions, chanting again and again on our own, I tried to match my inhales and exhales to the lines. By the time I made it to my mark, my breath was starting to even out. I lifted my shirt and wiped off the sweat that had started to bead on the tip of my nose.

My eyes were trained on my feet. I couldn't think about my hands.

I got in a few final stretches while my heart beat out like a drum.

Badoom! Badoom! Badoom!

I cracked my neck and my knuckles.

Then I took one last look around the track.

Laina in first leg.

Me in second.

Luce in third.

And Neeka . . . our anchor.

CLICK . . .

The sun beat down on the track in a harsh orange light.

CRACK . . .

I held my breath, just like always.

BOOM!

My body faced forward, but my head was turned back so I would know when to move. I could feel my legs tremble.

Laina was coming up strong, her hair whipping behind her side to side.

Breathe, Kam. Breathe.

I couldn't tell what place she was in. But as soon as she hit the fly zone, the mark that said I could blast off like a rocket, I only had seconds to turn my head back around in front of me and put my hand out. Then start running. And that all had to happen in one fell swoop, or I could lose the baton.

AGAIN.

Laina hit the mark. I shot my hand back and started running.

Air pushed out of my lungs like fast notes.

Here she is.

Here she is.

Here she is.

The cool metal baton landed hard in my palm, and I gripped it tight.

Tighter than anything I'd ever held onto in my life.

We nailed it!

I was in my rhythm now.

My heartbeat kept hammering away, while my lungs worked double time.

The track fell away.

My legs were cruising – first on air, then on clouds, then on stardust.

The freedom of flying.

I passed Pluto and was leaving the solar system.

That only lasted a split second, though.

Luce snatched me back to earth.

She was standing ahead of me, her tiny body pulled tight.

I hit my mark, and she whipped her hand back. Then she started running. I caught up to her and slapped the baton in her open palm.

Boom.

We stuck it again and off she went. Luce took tight to the curve and ran her little heart out. We were in second place. My heart skipped a beat.

This was about to be the last part. I hoped it would be the best part.

Boom.

The final handoff went off without a hitch.

Now Neeka had to do the chasing so she could catch up to first place.

She was going . . .

She was going . . .

Neeka was head-to-head with Crazy-Cold Eyes, her sneakers throwing off sparks.

I remembered Crazy-Cold Eyes taunting us. The sting of it.

Loser.

I thought of Alexis not being with us.

And Luce being with us for the last time.

My heart clenched.

Win or lose, this was it.

Everything was coming full circle.

I raised myself up on the tips of my toes and climbed

310

in place – willing Neeka to the finish line. Then it was over.

Gone . . .

Neeka zoomed right past her.

The crowd let out the loudest roar because everyone loved a close call.

And Neeka just beat the fastest girl in our universe.

Laina and I ran through the grass, still out of breath, with Luce not far behind us. Laina was squeezing my hand as hard as I was squeezing hers.

When Luce caught up with us, she hopped on my back.

Her voice vibrating as it came out. 'We . . . did . . . it!'

I bounced her up and down a few times before she got off.

The three of us held hands, jumping up and down.

The crowd was still cheering as Neeka swaggered over to us in bright beams of light, her eyes electrified. She stopped for a minute and bent over, putting her hands on her thighs and letting her head hang low. Then she got back in her stride. Her chest was all puffed up, as coaches and other runners tapped her shoulders and swatted her legs.

State champions.

77.
WHOA, NELLY!

Everything was blurry. Even the sun looked out of focus.

We stopped walking and flopped down on the grass, still breathing big.

The noise of the crowd faded to a distant, dull chatter.

It was still sinking in.

We did it.

We were state champions!

This was what we had been working for.

What I had been waiting for.

For two whole years!

'I know it's not the same without Alexis,' Laina said, still breathless as she stretched out on the grass. 'But we still won.'

Luce and Laina looked at each other and then at me.

'Laina,' I said smiling. 'It's exactly how it was supposed to be.'

Neeka sat up and shielded her face from the sun with

one hand. 'I second that emotion! Isn't that what you always sing Luce.' She was grinning hard.

Luce popped up. '*What?* Neeka's out here trying to be me. Now we really gotta celebrate.' She did a jig.

'Stop right there,' another voice said.

I looked up. Alexis was half-leaning on Shari, who must've helped her hobble over. One hand was on her hip. Momma-style. 'How are you starting the party without me?'

I jumped up quickly. 'We'd never start anything without you. You know that.'

'Good,' Alexis said, giving a perfectly huge smile and shaking her one good side.

'Whoa, Nelly!' Luce howled. 'You better sit down before you sprain the other half.'

A second later, I was back on the grass propping myself up on my elbows and tipping my head back towards the sky.

Shari sat down next to me and the six of us slipped into a kind of rhythm.

Not the same chitter chatter we usually had, but it sounded sweet all the same.

Luce sang in her real pretty voice, instead of her play one.

Alexis, Shari and Laina started talking about the rest of the meet and the last days of school, which were coming on fast.

A little later, Neeka elbowed me.

When I glanced over, our eyes locked. She looked

at me grinning and not uttering a single word and I knew in that moment we both felt connected to the same thing.

Something that didn't need saying at all.

78.
THE SOUND
OF ME

A little while later, Luce and I had our arms looped around each other's shoulders as we floated through the crowds. 'That,' she said, with a dizzy smile, 'was crazy.'

I smiled back. 'What part of it? Alexis falling or Laina running or us winning?'

'All of it!'

'Yup. It was out of this world!'

'Speaking of out of this world . . .' Luce said, pointing in front of us. I looked over to find Momma, Baba and Aunt Rose fast-walking over. Odie trailed a few steps behind looking shy. 'I'ma leave you.' She waved good-bye, stuck out her tongue, and ran off to find her people.

Aunt Rose made it to me first, sing-shouting.

When she waved her hands in the air, I saw she was holding the *kipepeo* kanga.

'We did it!' I said reaching out for her.

'We did, didn't we.' She hugged me tight and wrapped the kanga around my shoulders. I clasped the ends of it together at my chest. Holding the kanga tight with one hand and Aunt Rose with the other, I thought about what I'd just said.

We did do it.

It wasn't how I had expected things to turn out, and more people were a part of our winning than I could have imagined.

We'd added Laina to the mix.

And Alexis was still part of the win, even if she didn't run.

Aunt Rose, too.

Like the kanga draped over me now, it was like Aunt Rose was right over my shoulder, cheering me on every step of the way.

Suddenly, it all clicked.

From the time Aunt Rose first started talking to me about heartsongs, I had been listening really hard and hoping I'd find my familiar rhythm again. Then, in those quiet moments on the track, right before the race started, I heard something coming through.

I could feel it vibrating inside me, too.

A long stream of smoothness and roughness, and everything in between.

The scritch-scratch of my fight with Neeka.

The sweetness of making up with Odie.

Aunt Rose's sing-song stories.

And Laina's little hiccup laugh.

The silliness from Luce's jokes and Alexis's I-told-you-sos.

The chant's *clap, clap, clap* and the crashing baton's *clink, clank, clatter*.

The roar of winning. The wibble wobble woozy of losing, too.

I heard Momma and Baba's soft *shushshushshush* . . .

And my own steady *boom, boom, boom*.

The sound of me.

It wasn't perfect.

Or complete.

But it was still there, alive and thrumming.

Just like Aunt Rose said.

I guess I had to be open to hearing something new.

Something different.

A remix.

Aunt Rose stepped to the side and Momma and Baba pulled me in for a hug.

Baba quickly raised his eyebrows. Which was code for, 'Let's get moving and beat the traffic. We'll celebrate at home.'

Odie, who had been hanging back, waltzed over to me. The two of us followed behind Aunt Rose and Momma, while Baba used his brisk, long-legged stride to lead us back through the crowd to the car.

Odie shook his head. 'So, on a scale of one to ten, how freaked out were you when you saw Alexis crash?'

I chuckled. 'I started at a ten, but then I brought it down to a two.'

'Wow. I'm impressed. The Kam I know used to have a hard time handling a change in her afternoon snack.'

I made a face. 'Maybe I'm a different Kam.'

'OK. So, what are we gonna do with you now?'

'What do you mean?' I said a little louder, so he could hear me over the crowd.

'You're being calm and getting superhero capes and winning state meets in a single bound.' He lifted one end of the kanga and it floated in the air.

I laughed. 'Yeah, so?'

'So . . . I can see you getting big-headed.'

I stopped walking and shifted my stance, wrapping the kanga-cape tighter around my shoulders. 'You mean big-headed like you?'

A long second passed.

Odie's mouth hung open a little, like he was thinking. He squinted. 'I . . . uh . . . actually can't think of a comeback for that right now.'

'That's because there is no comeback for the truth.' I grinned, kept walking and dodging people.

'Wait a minute,' Odie said, a second later with an a-ha look on his face. 'You have an unfair advantage. Aunt Rose is like a secret weapon. She's making your wisecracks . . .' He looked up to the sky like he was searching for a word. 'Crackier!'

I laughed. 'She's helping me with a lot more than that. And how about she's just making my wisecracks wiser.'

'OK,' Odie said, raising his hands in surrender. 'Enough already. I have some serious work to do . . .'

'Yup!' I said as we stepped around strewn jerseys and discarded race numbers.

79.
DISASTER TIME

Aunt Rose had another rule in her house. On the days leading up to a big event, like a school exam or a Christmas play, her kids could rest and relax. They would be served and spoiled. Little was expected of them.

In other words, they could chill.

The day after the event, though, was another story. She wanted her kids to show their appreciation for all the support they'd received by cooking the family dinner.

That's how I found myself in the kitchen, overheated, doing the worst possible chore after the best day of my life.

'Hmph,' Aunt Rose snickered, looking at my posture. 'All that form on the track and none in the kitchen.' She was standing between the bewilderingly crammed island and the splattered stove, where I hunched over a wide pan of rice. An apron was tied around my waist, and my armpits were itchy from all the stress.

I continued stirring furiously fast.

Aunt Rose turned to me and gently pulled my shoulders

back. Then she took the wooden spoon from my hand and showed me the proper way to stir. 'Slow down, *kipenzi*. The race is over. And look . . .' She pointed the spoon at the tiles behind the stove. Bits of rice and peas speckled the wall. 'Let's try to keep it in the pot.'

'I am,' I groaned, as I poked at my underarm skin through my T-shirt.

'*Hehn!* You better wash your hands now. It's like you've never been in a kitchen other than to eat.' I hadn't, really. And who could blame me?

The kitchen door swung open, and Momma came bounding in from the hairdresser. Her hair was perfectly curled at the ends and bounced like she did. 'How is our little chef-in-training?' She smiled. 'Aunt Rose is a master. Even my food tastes better.' It didn't. But I didn't bother bursting her bubble.

While she hung her keys and purse on the hook by the door, I walked to the sink to wash my hands. I shook off the extra water and grabbed the tattered hand towel that hung from the kitchen cabinet door.

'I wouldn't get my hopes up if I were you,' I said, after a long moment. 'I've inherited none of Aunt Rose's genius cooking skills and I think one hundred percent of yours. It's disaster time over here.'

Momma sat down at the table. 'I survived on cereal for years and then married your father, a man who loves, and is now forced, to cook. I don't want you to end up like me.'

I went over to sulk on her lap. 'I already have.'

She squeezed my shoulders. 'You haven't. You have time to practise. And you, of all people, know what good practice can do.'

'Practice and patience and love,' Aunt Rose said in a gentle tone.

'But sometimes don't you just want something quick?' I asked. 'I mean, if you're in a rush or something.'

'Of course. Chapati only takes me forty minutes. That's quick. *Not so?*'

Momma and I laughed.

'Dar quick, maybe,' I said. Momma nodded her head in agreement.

'Up, up, up.' Momma swatted my behind. 'You have to get the hang of this and there is no one better to teach you. I'll start writing things down for the party.'

Momma and Baba had decided that we would have a party at the house on the last day of school to celebrate the end of the year, our big win, and Aunt Rose's visit.

Aunt Darien and the rest of Momma's friends would be there.

Even some of Baba's work colleagues.

I still had one more week of homework and exams.

But the party was the bright light at the end of the tunnel.

'So,' Momma said. She grabbed a pad of paper and a pencil from the bookshelf and was poised to take notes. 'Who are you inviting, and what decorations do you want? Aunt Rose and I have already discussed the food so you'll just have to let her know what to add.'

I walked back to the island and leaned over, placing my chin in my palms. 'Well, of course, Odie and the girls, including Laina.'

'Hello, good people!' The kitchen door swung open and an unusually cheery Baba waltzed in. He'd been working in his study. 'I'm almost done with my work and wanted to see how things were going.' His eyes carefully surveyed the surroundings. I'd made more of a mess than Aunt Rose ever had. He looked over at me. 'I can't believe we will eat a Tanzanian meal prepared by the inimitable Ms Kamaria Kessy herself.'

I straightened up and raised my chin. 'I've told Momma, and I'm telling you. Don't get your hopes up.'

Aunt Rose laughed. She'd been busy at the stove finishing up. 'I'm not just a good cook,' she said, turning to face the three of us. 'I'm also a wizard. I've already balanced out the flavours. Come and see.' She pointed at me with her mouth.

I moved closer to the stove, and she held the spoon to my lips while Baba sat down. 'I'm sure Saayande, Yaro and Tumo will be happy to have your food again,' he said to Aunt Rose.

I wheeled around to Baba so fast I almost gave myself whiplash. '*What?*'

80.
SILVERY
LINING

Wait, what? Did I just hear correctly? Was Aunt Rose leaving?

I couldn't believe my ears.

I never knew how long Aunt Rose was supposed to be staying.

Baba would've made a criminal case out of it if I'd asked again. So I never did after that first time, when he refused to answer.

But he'd made it seem like months.

I guess somewhere inside of me, I figured it might even be longer than that.

And now, just when I'd gotten used to her . . .

When I actually *loved* her being here . . .

When I couldn't imagine her *not* being here . . .

She was leaving.

I know I was supposed to be getting better at adjusting

to fast-changing rhythms, but this didn't seem fair.

I took a long breath and slowly sat down.

Baba kept his eyes on me. 'Yes, we didn't want to disturb you with this before your race. Aunt Rose is going back home at the beginning of July.'

'You guys really know how to drop bombs on me.'

Baba came behind me and put his hands on my shoulders. 'There's some good news, too.'

'What's that?' I asked, sinking down further into my chair and feeling shaky.

The room fell strangely silent.

I raised my head to find Momma, Baba and Aunt Rose circled around me.

'*What?*' I groaned, crossing my arms.

Baba had the cheesiest smile on his face. 'Aunt Rose is going back to Tanzania, but so are you!'

I must've still looked sour because Momma sat down at the table across from me and said, 'That was supposed to be good news, Kam.'

I cleared my throat. 'It was . . . It is. I'm . . . I just don't understand.'

'You'll have plenty of time to think later,' Aunt Rose said smiling. 'There's more.' She looked at Baba. 'Tell her.'

I braced myself.

Baba smiled. 'Momma and I are going, too. We're all going . . . together . . . as a family.'

I felt a smile starting at the edge of my lips. 'Really?' I looked from Momma to Baba. 'All of us?'

'Baba,' Aunt Rose said, in a low voice. 'You had better tell all. She doesn't like piece by piece.'

The news just got better. We were all going to Tanzania for a visit *and* Aunt Rose was planning to come back to Philadelphia. She'd decided that she wanted to go to school here. Art school. She was going home to get her affairs in order. She would leave a few weeks before us. We'd join a few weeks later and then she would come back to the US when all of her paperwork was done. Baba wasn't sure how long it would take for that to happen, but he said he was sure they'd get it sorted quickly since he knew exactly what to do. For once, Baba's job was useful! He waited until he was done sharing everything else before he sprang the best part on me. When Baba, Momma and I travelled to Tanzania in July to meet up with Aunt Rose and the rest of our family, Odie would come too. It would be our annual summer trip.

Before I got too swept up in the excitement, I had to ask Aunt Rose something. 'What about Saayande and the twins? Are they fine with you coming back here for school?' I wondered how my cousins would cope. I couldn't imagine being without Momma for months on end, never mind a year or however long it took to finish art school. And their father, who had long disappeared, was still nowhere to be found.

Aunt Rose's eyes softened. 'Yes, it's never easy when families are split apart. But remember those talks we've had about balance and sacrifice . . .' I nodded; I did. All of our talks were stored in my memory. I was surprised at how often I'd reached for them. 'In any case,' she went on, 'there's a silvery lining.'

Aunt Rose and her way of saying things. Just like Luce.

'What's the silvery lining?' I asked with a smile from deep in my soul.

'I'll be here. With you!'

'What's the first thing you'll do when you get home,' I asked Aunt Rose that night. The window was open and a warm breeze fluttered the curtains, finding its way to my leg which was poking out of my bed sheet.

Aunt Rose smiled. 'After hugging my *watoto*, I will head straight to the kitchen.'

I cracked a small smile back. 'Geez, Aunt Rose. More cooking?'

She angled to me and nodded.

'Lucky them,' I said, feeling a new wave of sadness wash over me. I'd have to prepare my stomach for Momma's cooking again.

I'd have to prepare my heart too.

Soon, it would have an Aunt Rose-shaped hole. At least, until she came back.

Aunt Rose sat up. 'Ah, *kipenzi,* don't worry. You will adjust.'

I sat up. 'How did you –?' And then I remembered who I was talking to. I huffed back onto my bed. 'I know, Aunt Rose. I'll still miss you.'

'I'll be back soon,' she said, plumping her pillow like she always did. 'But since I'm still here, let me tell you a story.' She put her head back down, her eyes twinkling, and smiled her secret smile. Her story smile. The special one that had lit up so many of our nights together. I pulled my knees into my chest and closed my eyes and took a slow breath, happy for now that this one thing hadn't changed . . . yet.

81.
AUNT ROSE STRIKES AGAIN

On Monday after school, I was sitting outside on the stoop watching Dacia braid her little sister's hair when I heard the door creak open. I turned around to find Baba hovering in the doorway.

'Catching the last of the Monday sunrays?' he asked, sitting down next to me.

I looked up and caught a bird wheeling against a stretch of sky. 'I guess.'

Baba put a hand around my shoulder and squeezed. He looked down at my foot, which was tapping up a storm. 'What's wrong?'

My nose wrinkled. 'Nothing. Just thinking.'

'About Aunt Rose?'

I nodded.

'And our trip to Tanzania?'

I nodded again.

Baba tapped his knee against mine. 'And being a state track champion?'

A small smile escaped from my lips. 'Yup.'

'And Luce leaving at the end of the summer?'

I looked over at him. 'How'd you remember that?' I was surprised he remembered Luce's leaving, but I shouldn't have been.

Baba had been around a lot more the last few weeks.

I had been right that spellbinding night. His big case *had* turned a corner.

Baba took my hand in his. 'I know I've been busy this past year. But it doesn't mean that I don't know what's happening.'

'And what about Odie?' he asked softly. 'Is the rift over?'

My face dropped. 'How did you know about that?'

There was a hint of a smile on Baba's lips. 'Odie is like a son to me. You think I wouldn't notice if he wasn't around here as much, telling his unfortunate jokes or forcing me to make wagers about the Bulls he's destined to lose? And I certainly noticed that you stopped sneaking down to call him on Thursdays after *A Different World*.' He raised an eyebrow sky high, still smiling.

I crossed my arms. 'Seriously, Baba. Why do you know all of this? It's so out of line.'

Baba kept his eyes on me. He tapped my forehead with a long finger. 'Because you are the blood of my blood. And because having Aunt Rose around has helped me, too. I'm going to try to slow down with work. Maybe help your mother with the cooking, too.' He gave me a slick grin.

I smiled to myself and shook my head, seeing so clearly in my mind, *Aunt Rose Strikes Again*, in bright electric blue comic book letters.

A few slow minutes passed.

Then a stream of birdsong filled the air like a bell, breaking the silence.

Baba lifted himself up, turning to me. His face lit up. 'How about a Carmichael's run with Odie right now?'

I smiled hugely. 'Yes!'

82.
TEAM DORITO
FOREVER

About a week later, at exactly 2:30 p.m., after the last bell rang, Alexis, Luce, Neeka *and* Laina met me at my locker. We walked down the hallway and got swept up in the whole student body pouring out of the double doors like a flood.

Odie beat us to the far side of the quad. He was standing under the archway by the time we got there. We folded him in and started walking over to my house.

Anybody with eyes could tell it was the last day of school.

We were finally free!

Our footsteps were airy and unhurried.

They were as soft as pitter-patters.

We were unbothered.

We didn't pay anyone any mind.

We joked and laughed down the sidewalk, our arms connected together like links of chain.

We nudged each other.

We jumped across the crosswalk, our bags finally light as feathers.

We were as light as feathers.

Warm air encircled us, tying invisible ropes around our arms and legs. Slowing us down even more. By the time we made it to the brownstone and floated up the steps, it felt like hours had passed. But it was only 2:45 p.m.

Everybody except Laina knew the drill.

We huddled in the entranceway and took off our shoes while Luce explained all about Momma and Baba's no shoes rule.

Laina followed suit.

The second we stepped into the house, we were embraced by the fragrant aroma of Dar spices. It was like a warm hug from Aunt Rose herself.

Bunches of balloons floating on strings filled the front hallway.

I grabbed a few and herded everyone towards the kitchen.

When I swung open the door, Aunt Rose was at her command station. A million steaming pots at her back. Flour-dusted island at her front. She wielded a rolling pin around like a magic wand. We trooped in all smashed together like a conga line, while Aunt Rose sang, 'The girls are here! The girls are here!' When she spotted Odie bringing up the rear, she shouted, 'The boy, too! The boy, too!'

I was stunned at Aunt Rose's appearance.

With her braids smoothed back in a tight bun, her spotless skin, and her shining eyes, she looked like she'd stepped right out of Teen Magazine.

And instead of the billowy print dresses she normally wore – which were more formal and hid how narrow she actually was – she'd put on blue jeans and a black and white polka-dotted button-down shirt. It was tucked in at the waist and rolled up at the sleeves. She looked nothing like the stranger I had in my mind weeks ago.

To be honest, she looked like one of us.

Momma was nowhere to be seen, but she must've left the kitchen stereo on.

It filled the room with sound.

It didn't take Luce a minute to move her feet while we stood crowded around the kitchen table. I introduced the girls to Aunt Rose again – *Baba-style* – since there'd only been time for fast, noisy hellos at the Night of Learning and the track meets.

Aunt Rose slid over and gave everyone a hug, one by one.

Even crazy dancing Luce, who she hugged while swinging her hips to match.

When she returned to her station, she pointed at Luce with the rolling pin. 'You,' she said with a serious look. 'You have African blood.'

Luce's feet were still moving in circles. She grinned. 'Yup, I do. Mamí always says so.'

Aunt Rose nodded her head in approval as she started to knead the dough in front of her. We grabbed handfuls of chips and popcorn from the table and tried not to leave too many crumbs. Between chomping and laughing, Alexis, Neeka, and I talked about our new favourite sneakers and the Barcelona Olympics starting in a few weeks.

Luce's feet finally stopped going berserk and she sat down.

Laina looked on, laughing and taking it all in.

'Wait,' Neeka busted out. 'I forgot to tell you something. I overheard Coach Rosse talking to Mr Guilfoyle yesterday.' Neeka paused for too many seconds while she grabbed more chips.

'Yeah, *AND*,' Alexis said impatiently. 'What about Coach and Patrol?'

'It's about these . . .' she said, chomping.

We all gave her a face. Laina, too.

'Spit it out,' I said.

'Hold up, let me finish my snack,' Neeka said.

Odie dipped into the conversation for a minute to say, 'If this is how you guys normally communicate, no wonder you've had issues.'

'A dictionary for the newbies might be nice,' Laina added, smiling.

'Don't worry, Laina,' Neeka said. 'We got you. Kam can whip that up. She's the one on words. But if you wanted –'

Alexis and I shouted, 'WHAT was it, Neeka?'

'Well,' she said, dragging the word out. 'You kind of had to be there.'

We all groaned.

'OK, OK,' she started. 'Coach Rosse was telling Mr Guil . . . I mean, Patrol, about the meet . . .'

'*Mmm hmm*,' we chorused.

'And he said with a slick grin, "My girls did great. They were all that *and a bag of chips*", to which Patrol replied, I KID YOU NOT, "Dixon, let me get this straight, are you comparing the track team to Lay's potato chips . . . or, perhaps, *Doritos*?"' Neeka dropped her jaw wide open. A stream of crunched chips tumbled onto the floor.

'Lemme get this straight,' Alexis said. 'Coach is trying to bite our style *and* scramble Patrol's brain at the same time? I can't . . .'

I crumpled into laughter.

Luce fell out. She went straight from her chair to the floor.

Feet up. Howling.

Coach Rosse was always making corny jokes and trying to be down.

This time he'd crossed a line.

Then again, it was the end of the year.

Maybe he was ready to let loose, too.

Either way, he'd made our day by embarrassing himself and then making Patrol embarrass himself even worse.

'OK, Dorito,' Luce said from down below, leaving off the 's' in her Luce way. Tears were streaming down her face from all the laughing.

'We're Team Dorito now,' Alexis said.

'Team Dorito forever!' Neeka shouted. She stood and pulled us all up one by one, even Luce who was still on the kitchen floor.

Then we circled ourselves like we'd done a bazillion times before, only this time with one more person, and with arms wrapped around each other's shoulders, shouted, 'Team DORITO forever!'

Our old circle and our new one, all at the same time.

Our old rhythm and our new one, too.

Odie and Aunt Rose looked on, smirking and shrugging.

The girls and I whooped it up even louder.

EPILOGUE

ONE MONTH LATER . . .

When the doorbell rang, I raced downstairs and threw the door open.

'That was fast,' Odie said, walking in.

'I told you I'm brand-new,' I said. 'I'm very respectful of other people's time now.'

He rolled his eyes, handing me a notepad and a pencil while he took off his shoes.

I gave him a look. 'What's this all about?'

He stood up, pushed his hair out of his face, then walked around me into the house. 'I'm taking notes. I've never packed for a trip to Africa before.'

'Well,' I said following behind him as he climbed the stairs up to my room. 'I don't have anything out of the ordinary in my suitcase to show you.'

He turned around. 'I'll be the judge of that.'

I scooted past him and into my room. I faced him. 'I want to show you something first.'

I sat on my bed with my legs crossed.

Odie sat across from me on the carpet.

I could see his foot tapping up a storm, which meant he was ready to tear through my suitcase, making sure I didn't have any unfair advantages on him by packing things for our trip he hadn't thought of, but I wanted to share Aunt Rose's letter first.

She gave it to me at the airport on the day she left for Tanzania.

It was folded into a new kanga that she'd pressed into my hands after a long hug.

Waves of people had streamed past us in the terminal while tears welled up in both of our eyes. Momma was so flustered by the commotion her face got all splotchy and red. Even Baba's eyes were wet, although he tried to hide it.

Thankfully, our trip to Dar was right around the corner.

I pulled the letter from under my pillow and read it to Odie, word for word:

Dear Kamaria,

Oh, how I have enjoyed my visit with you. I love Mama and Baba with all of my heart, but you made my first trip to America extra special. How could I have known that you would be so smart, so caring, so filled with fire and joy? How could I have known that you cherished family and friendships and heart connections just like

I do? I couldn't have known. You were a complete surprise. The best one. Here is a kanga to mark the end of the school year, the success you've had at your track meetings, and most importantly, your beautiful heartsongs. I can hear them now in my own heart. I am so proud of you. In the four weeks of my visit, I watched you grow taller. I also watched you stay exactly the same. That is the spirit of this kanga. It says:

HAPA UMEFIKA

In English:

You are here or This is the place you are looking for or You have arrived.

I love you,

Aunt Rose

I folded the letter back in half and set it down on the bed beside me. 'Isn't she the best?'

Odie shook his head. 'That's what I was trying to tell you. Unfair advantage.'

I laughed, thinking maybe he was right.

Weeks ago, when Aunt Rose arrived with her two suitcases, I had no idea she was bringing a whole new world, too.

A world filled with heartsongs and butterfly wings.

Being seen.

Seeing yourself.

Being yourself.

I thought about little Kam.

The one who was searching everywhere and anywhere for heartbeats.

Maybe she was hunting for something that never needed finding to begin with.

Because it wasn't out there.

It was right here, in me and around me, all along.

'So,' I said, smiling at Odie, who was still champing at the bit. 'After you ransack my suitcase, can I try to teach you a little Swahili?'

'Absolutely not,' he said, grinning.

I scooted to the edge of the bed, crossing my legs under me. 'I can't believe we're actually going to Tanzania. Aunt Rose says we're gonna love it.'

Odie crawled up next to me.

We were sitting side by side now.

I was pretty sure he could hear my heartbeat go *boom, boom, boom, boom*.

I unravelled my legs and let them hang over the bed.

I gripped the side of the bedframe.

Odie put his left hand on top of my right one. 'She's right, you know.'

I barely moved an inch. It took a few more seconds before I could turn my head to look him in the eye. 'Who?' I asked. 'Aunt Rose?'

'Yes, silly.'

I shrugged. 'Yeah . . . well I hope she's right and we love it.'

'No. Not about that.'

'Oh,' I said puzzled. 'About what, then?'

'What she said about you in the letter.'

'Which part?' I asked, still looking at Odie. He pushed his hair out of his eyes. They were shining like full moons. 'That I've grown or that I've stayed the same or that I found the place I was looking for?'

A small silence passed.

He looked me straight in the eye and squeezed my hand. 'Yup.'

I took a deep breath.

And just like that, I was soaring again.

ACKNOWLEDGEMENTS

I am indebted to Alice Sutherland-Hawes for being the first person to see something in this story and working assuredly to bring it to light. Many thanks to the team at David Fickling Books for helping me shepherd my debut middle-grade novel into the world, and especially to Rosie Fickling for her sharp editorial eye. Bex Glendining, thank you for channelling Kamaria's heart and fire in your brilliant cover illustration. You absolutely nailed it! I am grateful to Ayesha, Ciku and Jori, who read early drafts and offered themselves up as a community of writers with whom I could struggle and strive alongside. Eternal gratitude to my trusted confidante of twenty-three years, Marissa Arthurs, who reads all my writing at a nascent stage, and I hope always will. Aïcha Diallo, thank you for your fellowship and for always keeping me and my quiet writing spirit in mind. Love to Afua Ofosu-Barko and Yasmine Lonon for our sister circle and for your years of encouragement and support. Thank you to the Ugandan community in Boston during the 1980s and 1990s. In many ways, I understand my place in the world because of your grounding force, because you poured a community ethic into me, and because you created an environment of unmatched comedic relief (and dancing!). To the many friendships of my youth – Bonnie, Kristen, Laura, Melissa, Heather, Truc, Rosalie, Jody, Ayanna, Rhonda, Nikki – I remember! To HBH, the coach who pushed me to keep running. All these years later, I still am! A deep bow to my parents. *Mwebale nnyo, mwebalire ddala*. And to Birungi, Mutebi and Mukasa, my siblings-in-arms, and also Peera and Winnie, thank you for sharing my childhood, for being co-witnesses to the hilarity (madness), for showing up and showing me a good time still, and for the constant supply of jokes (silence!). Mom, Pop and Aaron – I appreciate you always being there. Nothing I write, including this book, would exist without my husband, Zachary Isdahl. Thank you, infinity (to borrow from the children). Munchie and Baki, you show me the way. You have my eternal love. *Asante sana*. To the continent, birthplace of our collective human story, I honour you. To my readers, I am grateful. This book is for you.